MYSTERY OF THE TOLLING BELL

Nancy becomes involved in a maze of mystery when she accepts an invitation from Mrs. Chantrey, a client of Mr. Drew, to vacation at her cottage in a picturesque seaside town. Carson Drew has promised to join his daughter, but fails to arrive. The alarming disappearance of Mr. Drew and the odd circumstances surrounding his rescue are only the start of a series of highly dangerous adventures for Nancy and her friends Bess and George.

Mrs. Chantrey's story about a nearby cliffside cave reputedly inhabited by a ghost intrigues Nancy and she decides to investigate. Several frightened townspeople claim to have seen an apparition and heard the weird sounds of a tolling bell just before water rushes from the cave. What Nancy discovers and how she outwits a ring of swindlers will thrill all admirers of the courageous young detective.

"This is what I had hoped to find!"
Nancy exclaimed.

NANCY DREW MYSTERY STORIES

Mystery
of the
Tolling Bell

BY CAROLYN KEENE

PUBLISHERS *Grosset & Dunlap* NEW YORK

A NATIONAL GENERAL COMPANY

LIBRARY OF CONGRESS CATALOG CARD
NUMBER: 73–2183
ISBN: 0–448–09523–8 (TRADE EDITION)
ISBN: 0–448–19523–2 (LIBRARY EDITION)

PRINTED IN THE UNITED STATES OF AMERICA

Contents

CHAPTER I

The Perfume Cart

"NANCY, aren't we almost at Candleton? I'm tired of riding."

An athletic-looking girl, with short dark hair and the boyish name of George Fayne, stretched wearily in the convertible as it sped toward the ocean.

Nancy Drew, eighteen and attractive, was driving. She shrugged her shoulders and breathed deeply of the tangy salt air. A gust of wind blew her reddish-golden hair across her eyes. Tossing it aside, she smiled at the two girls seated with her: Bess Marvin and George, who were cousins.

"A few more miles," Nancy replied. "But it's worth waiting for."

"You mean because of the mystery at Candleton?" Bess asked teasingly. She was blond and pretty. "Right now I'm more interested in food."

"You shouldn't be!" George said bluntly,

glancing at her cousin's slightly plump figure.

Nancy laughed. "We have to eat, calories or not. Perhaps we'll come to a fishing village where we can get some lobster."

The three girls, who lived in River Heights, were en route to Candleton on White Cap Bay. They had been invited to spend a brief vacation there as guests of Mrs. John Chantrey. She was a close friend and client of Nancy's father, a well-known lawyer. He was to meet the girls at her home in the small town.

"I think your father was smart to make the trip by plane instead of riding with us," Bess observed as the car swung around another sharp curve. "At least he won't die of starvation."

"This is really a business trip for Dad," Nancy said. "Poor Mrs. Chantrey was swindled out of a lot of money. Dad's trying to get it back."

"How did it happen?" George asked.

"Dad didn't tell me many of the details," Nancy replied. "But he did hint at mystery. Mrs. Chantrey is a lovely person. I hope we can help her."

"She runs a tearoom?" George inquired.

"Yes. Mrs. Chantrey opened a gift shop and tearoom to make a livelihood for herself after she lost most of her money."

"I was hoping the mystery at Candleton would be about something more romantic than money," Bess remarked in disappointment.

Nancy's eyes twinkled. "There's another mystery!" she said. "Mrs. Chantrey mentioned in her letter that ghostly and unexplainable things happen along the coast of White Cap Bay."

George was interested at once. "Are you going to work on that, too?"

"All three of us are!" was the reply.

Nancy's young life had been crammed with adventure. Daughter of an eminent criminal lawyer, she was unusually sensible, clever, and talented.

Mrs. Drew had died when Nancy was three years old and Hannah Gruen had become the Drews' housekeeper. The kindly woman was like a mother to Nancy and was constantly warning her to be cautious while solving mysteries.

"If the three of us can't solve the two mysteries—" Nancy began.

"Look!" Bess interrupted, pointing to a sign. "Fisher's Cove! We're coming to a town!"

The road curved and twisted, then abruptly a cluster of quaint, unpainted houses came into view. Fishnets were drying on lines in the back yards. Children stopped their play and stared at the car.

"Apparently few tourists come into town this way," Nancy commented, steering carefully to avoid a street peddler who carried a basket of fish on his head. "We seem to be curiosities!"

The girls looked hopefully for a place to eat.

As Nancy turned left onto Main Street, they saw two hotels and several restaurants. Bess noted a sign with the name Wayside Inn and an arrow pointing up a narrow lane.

"Let's go there," she suggested.

Presently they came to a freshly painted, white house overlooking the surf. It proved to be cool, clean, and inviting. Although it was late for luncheon, the woman in charge assured the girls she could serve them.

The trio found the meal very appetizing. In addition to lobster and puffed shrimp there were tomatoes, coleslaw, potatoes, hot biscuits, lemonade, and apple pie.

"I know I've gained a dozen pounds!" Bess moaned as they paid their bill and left the inn.

"I feel like a puffed shrimp myself!" groaned George. "Let's walk around Fisher's Cove awhile for exercise before we drive on."

Although eager to reach Candleton, Nancy agreed to the suggestion. They took a path which led from the sandy shore to the shopping area of the village.

Here the girls found an interesting combination of the old and the new. An ancient surrey rattled past, drawn by a tired-looking white horse. The reins were held by an elderly man with a long, flowing beard.

Then a high-powered sports car sped by, a pretty girl at the wheel. Natives were a striking contrast to members of the summer colony who wore scanty beach clothes.

"Look!" cried Nancy suddenly as the girls reached a corner. "Isn't that attractive?"

From a side street came the musical tinkle of a bell. Then a dark-haired, heavy-set woman pushing a flower-decked cart came into view. Seeing the girls, she moved briskly toward them.

"Wonder what she's selling," Bess said in an undertone.

Dangling from a wire stretched between two poles on either side of the cart were strings of tiny red metal hearts and a little bell. The woman, who looked to be of foreign birth, wore a red skirt and white blouse with a large red heart embroidered on one sleeve. As she came alongside the girls, she addressed them in a torrent of words.

"You buy from Madame? I sell all zese articles for beautyment. Come see." She held up a bottle of perfume, some face powder, and a lipstick. Then she rolled her eyes and smiled. "Zese products make mademoiselle adored by the boy friend!"

Bess, intrigued by the display of cosmetics, fingered a large heart-shaped compact.

"Very chic—very cheap," the woman said in a singsong voice. "Seven dollars, please."

"But I don't wish to buy," Bess stammered, putting the compact back on the cart.

"You like better the perfume?" Before Bess could retreat, the woman had uncorked a tiny heart-shaped flask which she waved beneath Bess's nose. "One drop of this, and piff! The boy friend is yours!"

By this time a large number of persons had gathered about the cart. Many in the crowd were young girls.

"Just like in New York," Madame announced proudly. "Sold only in the best salons."

"I don't recall seeing the brand name before," Nancy remarked, observing that all the cosmetic containers bore the French words *Mon Coeur*.

"It means 'my heart,'" translated Madame.

"How much?" inquired a rather unattractive, large-boned girl with blond hair.

The woman named a high figure.

"That's a lot of money," the blond girl commented.

"I give you demonstration to go with it."

Madame took the bill offered her, then quickly applied the cosmetics to the girl's face. The woman's sales talk convinced other bystanders. They bought the Mon Coeur products freely, while the blond girl walked to a shopwindow and looked in the side mirror. To the surprise of Nancy and George she liberally put on more of the cosmetics. Then, apparently satisfied but vulgarly conspicuous, she went down the street.

Bess was intrigued by Madame and could not

Madame snatched the money.

resist the temptation to buy. "I'll take a small bottle of perfume," she decided.

"Bess!" remonstrated George. "You don't know a thing about Mon Coeur products!"

"My things are of the finest," Madame retorted.

"Bess, do come away," Nancy urged.

Quick as a flash Madame thrust the bottle into Bess's hand and snatched the money the girl had taken from her purse.

"Is this perfume the same as in the sample bottle?" Bess asked.

"They all the same," snapped the woman. She quickly gave Bess the change, then hurriedly walked down the street with her cart.

In her haste to get away, Madame cut directly across the road. The little bell jangled and the heart-shaped decorations swung back and forth.

At the same time the surrey with the old white horse which the girls had seen earlier jogged down the street. Its driver dozed at the reins. Suddenly a car backfired, frightening his mare. She gave a startled snort. Before the elderly driver realized what was happening, the animal bolted straight toward the woman and her cart!

With a scream of terror, Madame abandoned the cart and raced for safety. The horse plunged along wildly, pulling the surrey over the curb, then back into the roadway again. All the pedestrians had run for cover.

The flower-decked cart stood in the middle of

the street, directly in the path of the runaway horse. Nancy darted out and wheeled the cart to safety. An instant later the horse flashed by. Not until the mare had gone another block did the driver regain control.

"Nancy, you might have been killed!" Bess cried out. She was trembling.

"It was a courageous thing to do, but silly!" George said. "Madame's cosmetics aren't worth the risk you took!"

"I agree with you," Nancy said, parking the cart under an awning. "I acted impulsively."

"Let's go!" George urged.

Without waiting for Madame to return, the three friends started to cross the street. As Nancy stepped from the curb an excited woman rushed up and seized her arm.

"You're the one!" she screamed. "I'm goin' to have you arrested!"

Startled, Nancy retreated a step. But the stranger held tightly onto her arm.

"You're a thief, and you've got no business in this town!" she shouted. "You've ruined my daughter and taken her money! Police! Police!"

CHAPTER II

An Intriguing Story

NANCY pulled herself free from the excited woman. By this time Bess and George, seeing that their friend was in difficulty, darted to Nancy's side.

"Police! Police!" the woman screamed again. "My daughter's been robbed!"

"Who is your daughter?" Nancy asked her.

"You should know! You sold her that stuff to put on her cheeks and lips and eyelids! It made her look like a freak!"

Nancy now understood. "Then your daughter is one of the girls who bought several things from Madame with the cart."

"That's right. The big blond girl," the woman replied, "and it's you she bought them from. You needn't look so innocent! I saw you wheeling that cart when the horse ran away!"

Nancy explained that Madame sold the cosmetics, not she. Bess and George supported her story, but the woman would not listen.

"I want my money back!" she stormed. "My husband and I saved it up raisin' chickens. We gave Minnie fifteen dollars to buy a pair o' shoes and some other things she needed. Then along you come with that awful stuff and rob her! What's worse, you encourage her to paint herself up like an Indian warrior! I'll have the law on you!"

By this time a group of curious onlookers had gathered about them.

"Oh—oh, here comes a policeman!" George muttered to Nancy.

"What's going on, ladies?" the patrolman asked as he hurried up to the group.

"This girl robbed me!" the woman accused Nancy.

"That is untrue, Officer. This woman has mistaken me for someone else," Nancy said quietly.

"Then where is the other person?" demanded Nancy's accuser.

The girls turned to gaze toward the spot where they had left the cart. It was gone! Madame must have taken it away.

"I want my money back!" the woman resumed her tirade.

"See here," the policeman said sternly, "you're

creating an unnecessary disturbance. Exactly what is your charge against this young lady?"

"That she sold my daughter a lot of worthless things the girl doesn't need!"

At that moment a man stepped up to the group, introduced himself as Professor Atkins, and said he had seen the whole episode from down the street. Smiling at Nancy, he told how she had saved the flower-decked cart and had not received so much as a thank-you from its owner.

The woman turned pale. "I—I guess I've made a mistake," she muttered.

She retreated hastily. Nancy thanked the professor. Then, eager to leave, she quickly led the way to her car and drove out of town.

En route to Candleton, Bess opened the bottle of Mon Coeur perfume she had bought. After she had sniffed the perfume, the girl gazed at her companions a bit sheepishly.

"I'm afraid I was gypped," she said. "This isn't as good as the sample."

"It's fragrant, anyway," Nancy remarked as Bess held the bottle under her friend's nose.

Then George sniffed at the bottle. "Take my advice and throw it away."

"And waste all my money?" Bess recorked the bottle. "No. I'll keep it."

The road no longer offered the monotonous scenery it had on the other side of Fisher's Cove. Instead it ran lazily along moors carpeted with low-growing juniper, and at points the rocks split into colorful masses over which the sea's filmy spray leaped playfully.

"We're not far from Candleton now," Nancy declared as cliffs loomed in the distance.

The car rounded a sharp bend, and the girls caught their first glimpse of White Cap Bay. Never before had they seen such a stretch of beautiful water. Once only a fishing town, the little village of Candleton was now a fashionable summer resort with gleaming white cottages and fine hotels.

Mrs. Chantrey's attractive home stood some distance from the beach, just beyond the business section of the town. Nancy pulled to a stop in front of the house.

A woman about fifty opened the door, and smilingly said that she was June Barber and lived with Mrs. Chantrey. She helped the girls carry their luggage to the guest room, and explained that her friend was at the tearoom. Mrs. Chantrey had left word that the visitors were to make themselves at home.

"Has my father arrived?" Nancy asked.

"Not yet," June replied.

"I guess he was delayed," said Nancy, hoping that nothing was wrong.

"Let's go down to the tearoom," George suggested.

The girls quickly changed their clothes and

set out, taking a short cut that led directly to the beach. Wandering slowly along the waterfront, they saw many old-time fishermen's houses which had been converted into artists' studios. Men and women sat in the dazzling sunlight, sketching the boats which lay at anchor in the bay.

"What can the mystery be that's disturbing Candleton?" Nancy mused. "Everything seems very peaceful here."

"Yes, it does," Bess agreed.

Presently the girls saw Mrs. Chantrey's tearoom, the Salsandee Shop. Bright-colored umbrellas dotted its outdoor dining area and garden. Every chair was taken.

"What a clever name Salsandee is!" Bess observed, after Nancy explained the tearoom specialized in salads and sandwiches. "What does the 'dee' stand for?"

"I don't know. We'll have to ask Mrs. Chantrey."

The girls went inside. They were delighted by the cozy decor and the beautiful flower candles on the tables. The room was just as crowded as the garden.

A harassed waitress moved swiftly about, trying to take a dozen orders. Nervous and confused, she showed her annoyance as Nancy stopped her to inquire for Mrs. Chantrey.

"She's in the kitchen," the girl replied, "but

please don't bother her now unless it's important. Two of our girls failed to show up today, and we're nearly frantic trying to serve everyone."

"Why don't we pitch in and help?" Nancy suggested to her friends. "We've waited on tables before!"

"It would be fun!" agreed George.

In the kitchen, they found their hostess frantically making dozens of salads. Mrs. Chantrey, a woman in her mid-forties, was ordinarily a serene and well-groomed person. Now a wisp of gray hair tumbled down over one eye, and a splotch of salad dressing stained her apron.

"Hello," Nancy said cheerfully. "Do you need any help?"

Mrs. Chantrey dropped a knife. Her face mirrored dismay. "Why, it's Nancy Drew, and these are your friends!" she gasped. "How ashamed I am to be found in such a state!"

"You need help and we're here to give it," Nancy said with a smile. "Just tell us what to do."

"I can't put you girls to work the first moment you arrive! Why, you're my guests!"

"We'd like to do it," Bess spoke up.

"Then I won't protest any longer. You're a gift straight from heaven! If you can help out for an hour, the worst of the evening rush will be over."

Chatting excitedly, Mrs. Chantrey tied aprons on the three girls. While George remained in the kitchen to make sandwiches, Nancy and Bess were sent to wait on tables. They went to Dora, the waitress they had met a few minutes earlier, and requested instructions.

"You take the tables out in the garden," the girl directed Nancy. "Bess and I will handle the inside dining room. Here are your order pads. Don't try to carry too many dishes or you may have an accident."

"Waitress!" called an impatient voice.

"Everyone is in a dreadful mood," Dora whispered. "Some have been waiting nearly an hour for their food."

Nancy moved swiftly among the tables assigned to her. She took orders efficiently, learning the names of the dishes which made the Salsandee Shop so popular, including the Dandee Tart, filled with steaming hot fish pudding topped with salmon-colored meringue. The girls learned that the last syllable of the name Salsandee was derived from the "dee" in Dandee.

Customers, at first impatient and cross, soon began to smile. One of the last diners in the garden was a white-haired man with spectacles. He dawdled over a frosted glass of iced tea. Nancy hovered near, hopeful that he would leave, but instead he became talkative.

"Do you live here?" he inquired.

"No, I'm just a visitor, helping out," Nancy explained. "Actually I'm not a waitress."

"Well, I'm a stranger to this town myself. Came here looking for a bell."

Nancy remained politely silent.

"Not an ordinary bell, but one that was made in a casting furnace in Boston during the Revolutionary War. A Paul Revere bell—that's what I'm after."

"Are you an antique collector?" Nancy asked, becoming interested.

"Not exactly. Although, of course, old bells are valuable as antiques." The man gazed at her with shrewd eyes. "They tell me there are any number of old bells to be had around this town."

"I wouldn't know about that," Nancy replied. "I arrived here only a few hours ago."

"I see, I see," muttered the stranger. He finished his iced tea, left a coin by his plate, then went down the path toward the ocean.

While thinking about her conversation with the man, Nancy began to clear away the dishes. She dropped the coin into her pocket, intending to give it and the other tips to Dora.

As Nancy picked up a plate, she noticed a folded piece of paper on the ground at her feet and brushed it aside. Then the thought struck her that the paper might be important. Perhaps the diner who had just left the garden had dropped it.

Nancy picked up the paper. The handwriting on it was very old-fashioned. A puzzled look came over the young detective's face as she read the words, which were in French.

"*Whoever finds this may become enormously wealthy,*" she translated in amazement. "*In one of my XXX cast bells are embedded many jewels.*"

The paper had been torn in half, and the remainder of the strange message was missing!

CHAPTER III

Ghost in the Cave

As Nancy reread the mysterious words, Bess Marvin approached the table.

"Thank goodness the last customer has gone!" she exclaimed, pulling off her apron.

"Uh-huh," Nancy replied, her mind on the strange message.

"You're not listening!" Bess accused. "What is it you're reading, Nancy?"

"A paper I found on the ground after one of my customers left. He was an elderly man, Bess, and he said he had come to Candleton to find a bell that had been made by Paul Revere!"

Nancy handed the paper to her friend to read and waited for her comments.

"Do you suppose the man thinks the gems are hidden in the Revere bell? Why, it's another mystery, Nancy!"

"Not so loud," the young detective warned

with a quick glance around her. "If the contents of this paper should become known, some dishonest person in Candleton might start buying all the old bells around and selling them at a fancy profit."

"What is an XXX bell, Nancy?"

"I don't know, but my guess is the three X's might be the trademark of the maker."

"Wouldn't it be marvelous if we could find one ourselves!"

"That's an idea," Nancy said with a smile as she folded the paper. "We should return this to the customer who lost it. I wish I knew his name."

Neither Dora nor Mrs. Chantrey could provide any information about the elderly man. They were sure he had never been to the Salsandee Shop before.

"If the paper is valuable and belongs to him, he'll come back here to look for it," Nancy reasoned.

Mrs. Chantrey sealed the message in an envelope and dropped it into a desk drawer, instructing Dora to give it to the stranger should he call. Then, grateful to the girls for their efficient help, she insisted they stop work and return to her house.

"I'll go with you," she declared. "Dora will be able to take care of the few customers who may drop in between now and closing time. But first we'll have some dinner."

The moon was rising as the three girls later walked along the beach with their hostess. Farther up White Cap Bay they glimpsed a lighthouse, and Mrs. Chantrey pointed out Whistling Oyster Cove and Bald Head Cliff.

"Such picturesque names!" George remarked, stooping to pick up an odd-shaped shell. "Is fishing the chief occupation here, Mrs. Chantrey?"

"I'd say the making of salt-water taffy is!" She chuckled. "But seriously, there's one interesting spot you must visit," Mrs. Chantrey went on. "Mother Mathilda's Candle Shop."

"Did those lovely ones at the Salsandee Shop come from there?" Bess inquired.

"Yes. You may have noticed they're lightly perfumed."

As Bess and George asked questions about the village and its inhabitants, Nancy remained unusually quiet. She was concerned about her father's absence. Deep in thought, she was startled when her hostess suddenly asked about him.

"When will Carson arrive in Candleton, Nancy? We were expecting him this morning."

"I thought he'd be here before us," she replied. "Dad telephoned before I left River Heights and said he was taking a plane from New York."

Although Mr. Drew was a busy man, and Nancy realized that he might have been delayed by unexpected business, he had never failed to let her know of a change in plans.

"Now don't worry about your father," Mrs. Chantrey said quickly. "Perhaps there's a message at home."

Nancy brightened at the suggestion. But when they reached the house, June Barber said that no word had come. Even though Nancy was greatly concerned, she decided that she could not allow worry over her father's absence to spoil the evening for Bess and George.

"Tomorrow we must explore White Cap Bay," she said. "Mrs. Chantrey, in your letter you mentioned a mystery along the shore."

Her hostess smiled. "It concerns the cave at the base of Bald Head Cliff. My advice to you would be to avoid the spot."

"Please tell us why," Nancy urged.

"I've never been there myself," Mrs. Chantrey continued, "but townspeople say it's spooky and dangerous. According to the tale, Bald Head Cave is inhabited by a ghost. I don't believe in ghosts, but the fact remains that some unhappy accidents have occurred in that area. Several persons nearly drowned, and one man lost his life."

"How do the accidents happen?" Nancy asked.

"It's said the ghost causes water to rush out of the cave. He tolls a warning bell whenever people are near, and if they don't leave at once, the water engulfs them."

Bess shivered. "If the ghost were human, he'd drown too. So the thing must be supernatural."

"How long has this been going on?" Nancy asked.

"I don't know exactly," Mrs. Chantrey replied. "But not for long. From what I hear, I judge the cave has always been there, but not the ghost nor the rushing water nor the tolling bell."

"Has the cave been explored?" George asked.

"A few venturesome men have tried it but learned nothing."

The story excited Nancy's curiosity. She thought about it late into the night, and concluded there must be some logical explanation for the phenomenon. As Nancy dropped off to sleep, she told herself that the only way to find out was to go there herself and investigate.

In the morning, however, Nancy forgot about exploring the cave. No message had come from her father and she was unable to hide her alarm. She called her home in River Heights. Hannah Gruen had heard nothing from Mr. Drew and she in turn became worried.

A call to the lawyer's office brought no reassurance. Mr. Drew's secretary was on vacation, and the girl who was taking her place said she thought he had gone to Candleton.

"And there was no word from New York?"

"None at all."

Discouraged, Nancy thanked her and hung up.

"Perhaps he's been in an accident," she told her friends.

"Now do stop worrying, Nancy," Bess said kindly. "If your father had been in an accident, someone in River Heights would have been notified."

"Your father will be along any time now, so stop building up gory pictures," George cut in. To get Nancy's mind off the matter, she added, "How about exploring Bald Head Cave this morning?"

"All right," Nancy agreed with forced cheerfulness. "I wonder how we reach the place."

They learned from June that even at low tide the only safe approach to Bald Head Cave was by motorboat. When she realized the girls intended to go there, June warned them not to venture near the cave. Nancy assured her they would be careful. She and her friends left the house and rented a sturdy craft from a fisherman at a nearby boathouse.

Under Nancy's guidance the small boat put-putted slowly along the shore. Rising above the water, and stretching out for about two miles, were the colorful cliffs which had attracted artists from all parts of the country.

"I see a man up on that cliff with a telescope," George said, scowling. "He's looking at us. I hate people with telescopes. They have an unfair advantage!"

Nancy laughed as she steered nearer shore.

"No doubt summer visitors are resented by the all-year inhabitants."

The man disappeared from view as the boat came into the shadow of the cliff.

"Look! The entrance to the cave!" George cried as they reached an indentation about half a mile from the ocean. "It's rather large."

"Let's just explore the outside," Bess suggested nervously.

Nancy smiled as she switched off the boat's motor, allowing the craft to drift closer to shore. "You know very well, Bess, we couldn't learn a thing without going inside the cave."

"Besides, the story must be exaggerated," George added. "I don't believe in ghosts."

Bess, whose gaze had been focused steadily on the cave entrance, suddenly gripped her cousin's arm.

"What is it?" George whispered.

For a moment Bess, badly shaken, could not speak. Then, with a trembling hand, she pointed toward the dark mouth of the cavern and said shakily:

"The ghost! I saw its white robe. It—it went back into the cave!"

Startled by Bess's words, Nancy and George gazed toward the cave entrance. They could see nothing but the dark opening framed by rocks and water.

"You must have imagined it, Bess," declared George. "There's no ghost—nothing white."

"Not now, but it was there!"

"What did it look like?" Nancy asked.

"I saw only a white blur. But then, ghosts aren't supposed to have a regular form."

"You probably mistook a sea gull for a ghost." George laughed.

Bess's lips drew into a thin, stubborn line. "It certainly was not a bird," she insisted. "But forget it. Even if that cave were inhabited by twenty ghosts, I know I couldn't talk you two out of exploring it!"

Nancy had no intention of venturing farther in a reckless manner. As the boat drifted closer, she studied the entrance to the cave and listened intently.

"Hear any warning bell?" George asked jokingly.

Nancy shook her head. The only sound was the roar of the ocean in the distance.

"What's your plan?" George inquired.

"The cave is quite wide and if the water is deep enough we can row the boat inside," Nancy replied. From the bottom of the craft she picked up the lead line and began to take soundings at the entranceway. "The water is nearly two feet deep here," she announced, measuring the wet section of the line. "Our boat can't go aground."

Using the oars, the girls cautiously rowed

through the cave entrance into the dark interior. Nancy, who always carried a flashlight with her, swept its beam over the jagged stone walls. There was a natural ledge on one side, etched in the rock by erosion. The walls were damp, and the temperature much lower than on the sunny bay.

"It seems like a very ordinary cavern," commented George, relaxing. "No ghost. No bell. No water pouring out."

Nancy maneuvered the boat to the ledge and fastened the painter securely to a jagged piece of rock.

"What are you going to do?" Bess demanded.

"I want to walk along the ledge for a short distance. This cave may have an inner room. It's too dark to tell from here, and if we take the boat much farther, we may have difficulty getting out."

Bess was reluctant to leave the craft, but when she saw that George intended going with Nancy, she too climbed out on the ledge.

Nancy's roving flashlight cut dancing patterns on the water-stained walls as the three girls moved cautiously along the narrow ledge.

"I'm not going on!" Bess announced suddenly, turning and hurrying back toward the boat.

"Well, how about it, Nancy?" George inquired dubiously. "This place is—"

Her gaze was fixed on a portion of the ledge far back in the cave.

"The ghost!" she whispered tremulously. "I saw it just then—a figure in white!"

Nancy had observed nothing, but George's fear increased her own growing uneasiness.

"We'll go," Nancy agreed.

The two girls walked rapidly along the ledge toward the entrance. They had taken scarcely a dozen steps when a bell began to ring far back in the cave. Loud and full in tone, the pealing held a mournful note as if tolling for departed spirits.

Electrified by the sound, Nancy and George stopped suddenly. The same terrifying thought came to each of them.

"The warning bell Mrs. Chantrey told us about!" cried George. "It rings just before water rushes through the cave!"

Nancy seized her by the hand. "Come on!" she urged. "We must get out of here—fast!"

"Listen!" George cried tensely. "That roaring sound! Hear it?"

Both girls froze to the spot, for the sound they heard was the mad rush of a great wall of water plunging toward them with the speed of an express train.

"Run!" screamed Nancy. "Run for your life!"

CHAPTER IV

Nancy Vanishes

THE boat was still some distance away, tied to the jagged rock. Nancy knew that she and George never could reach it before the water struck them. But Bess, who stood on the ledge of the cave beside the craft, might escape.

"Get in the boat! Cast off!" Nancy shouted frantically.

It took Bess only a second to realize her great danger. She bent down to loosen the rope.

The next instant the great wall of water rushed through the cave, sweeping everything before it. Nancy and George, struggling desperately, were engulfed.

Instinctively Bess clung to the painter of the boat. As the water struck her, the rope snapped free of the rock. The craft raced toward the cave entrance.

Bess, holding fast to the rope, was carried face downward through the torrent.

Almost suffocated, Bess clung with all her strength to the rope as the boat shot from the mouth of the cave. Finally, when the speed of the craft lessened, she was able to raise her head to take a deep breath of air and grasp the gunwale.

The motorboat was half-filled with water. Bess knew if she climbed aboard, it probably would sink. Swimming with one hand, the girl tried to tow the boat toward shore. It was difficult going.

Frantically her eyes darted toward the cave entrance. Water still boiled from the cavern's gaping mouth. What had happened to her friends?

"Nancy! George!" she shouted.

There was no answer. Bess did not try to call out again. She concentrated all her efforts upon reaching the rocky beach.

Presently her feet struck bottom. Standing upright, she pulled the boat in so it could not float away, and began bailing water. As she worked, the distressed girl kept scanning the bay, hoping she might see Nancy or George.

"They're both good swimmers. I'm sure they reached safety," she told herself hopefully.

But in a moment panic seized her again. Possibly the girls had not been swept from the cave. They might have been caught inside and drowned!

Her mind numbed by fear, Bess worked automatically on the boat, hardly taking her gaze from the water. She suddenly detected an object some distance away. Could it be a swimmer?

Leaping to a high rock, Bess shaded her eyes against the glare of the sun. Yes, someone was swimming feebly. Even as she looked, the person disappeared.

"Hold on! Don't give up!" she shouted as the swimmer reappeared. "I'll reach you in a minute, George."

Bess rushed to the boat and tried to start the motor. It was waterlogged and refused to catch. The oars had been washed overboard. After kicking off her shoes, Bess plunged into the water.

"I'm coming!" she screamed.

Bess reached her cousin not a moment too soon.

"I'm—all—in," George gasped. "Hurt my arm."

Bess, realizing the other girl could no longer help herself, grasped her in the cross-chest carry and pulled her through the water. But it seemed as if she could not possibly reach the shore. Burdened by George's weight, and with her own strength giving out, she found it harder and harder to keep going.

But just as Bess was about to give up in despair, her feet came in contact with the bottom. Standing up, she discovered that the water was only a little above her waist.

Bess pulled the exhausted George to safety. It

was several moments before either of them could speak. Finally George mumbled:

"Nancy— Is—she—safe?"

Fear for their missing friend drove Bess into a panic. Anxiously she looked about. Nancy was not in sight.

When Bess did not answer, George tried to pull herself to a sitting position. But it was useless. Her strength was gone, and her left arm, bruised on the rocks when she had been catapulted from the cave, hung limp.

"Nancy—was—beside me—in the cave," she said brokenly. "That was the last I saw of her."

Tears rolled down the cheeks of both girls. Each was silent with her own thoughts. Then suddenly Bess sprang toward the motorboat. She was just in time to prevent the rising tide from carrying it down White Cap Bay. As Bess tied the rope to a rock on the shore, she was startled to hear a faint "Hello" from the direction of the cliff above the cave.

"Nancy's voice!" she exclaimed joyfully. "She's safe! But where?"

Excitedly calling a reply, she and George waited eagerly for another shout. But it did not come. Bess waded into the water and looked up. Nancy was seated high on the cliff among the rocks.

"There she is!" Bess cried out. "Thank goodness!"

Relieved, George felt her strength returning. She got up, and together the girls shouted reassuringly to Nancy. But she did not seem to see or hear them. How were they to reach her?

"We'll have to use the boat," George decided. "Where are the oars?"

"Gone. And the motor won't start," Bess said forlornly. "But maybe I can dry it off."

In a watertight compartment under one of the seats she found a few dry rags which she used to wipe off the engine parts. After several sputters the motor finally started and the girls were able to get under way.

"Now where's Nancy?" Bess asked, steering toward the mouth of the cave and looking up.

Their friend had disappeared!

Shouting her name several times, the cousins cruised back and forth near the base of the cliff. Nancy, however, did not reappear.

"She may have found a road up there and decided to hitchhike or walk to the boathouse," George decided at length. "Let's go back."

Upon reaching the boathouse, the girls saw Nancy's car parked exactly where it had been left a few hours earlier. Their friend was not there, and the fisherman from whom they had rented the boat reported that she had not returned.

The man looked hard at the girls. Although the hot sun had dried their clothing, they presented a

very bedraggled appearance. They replied briefly
to the fisherman's questions, but did not reveal
all the details of their mishap at Bald Head Cave.
They thanked him for the use of the boat, paid
him for it and also for the lost oars. Then they
left.

"We must find Nancy," George declared
anxiously. "Let's take the car and drive to the
cliff. We may meet her on the road." Fortunately
she knew where Nancy kept an extra key to the
automobile.

"But what about your arm?" Bess objected.

"It feels much better," George declared. "The
numbness is gone now. I can move it."

Meanwhile, Nancy was making an effort to recover from her own frightening experience. The
great rush of water had washed her out of the
cave just behind George. Being a strong swimmer,
she made her way back to the cliff and struggled
to a handhold amid the rocks some distance from
the entrance of the cave.

She pulled herself out of the water, and for a
time lay panting on the rocks. Then, getting to
her feet, she looked about in search of her friends.
The uneven line of the cliff obscured her view,
and she could not see Bess or George.

After shouting their names several times,
Nancy climbed higher. From this perch, she saw
the motorboat and both girls on the shore. Relieved that they were safe, she tried to figure out

a way to reach them. She decided to climb to the top, in the hope that she could find a path that would lead down to her friends. When Nancy reached the top, she stood still to look around. Suddenly she began to feel light-headed and had to sit down.

"I'm getting to be a sissy," she scolded herself. "I must go on."

But Nancy seemed unable to move from the spot. She became so drowsy she had to lie down. The warm sun and a faint sweet aroma added to her drowsiness. Delightfully comfortable, she lost all track of time.

Then, as if from a long distance away, Nancy thought she heard voices. Two men seemed to be arguing violently. Or was she dreaming?

Pulling herself up to a sitting position with great effort, Nancy gazed about her. She could see no one.

Then she fell back and drifted off into unconsciousness.

CHAPTER V

A Warning Message

DEEP in slumber, Nancy dreamed that she lay cushioned upon a soft, sweet-smelling meadow. Nearby a flock of sheep grazed peacefully, and the faint tinkle of bells came to her ears.

Presently two little brown elves crept from beneath a bush and stared at her as if she were an intruder. Nancy heard one of them say:

"We can't allow her to stay here."

"We certainly can't," agreed the other elf, whose voice was deeper. "We must move her before she wakes up."

Nancy tried to resist, but the elves seemed to have cast a spell over her. Powerless to move, she attempted to open her eyes but the lids felt as heavy as stones.

Borne upon the shoulders of the elves, she was carried a long distance. Then they put her down, but the couch was not a comfortable one. Something sharp cut into her back. Nancy rolled over, and suddenly was wide awake.

Sitting up, she gazed about her in bewilderment. Her clothing had dried in the sun but was very crumpled, reminding her of the struggle she had gone through to keep from drowning.

Nancy listened for the roar of the surf but all was quiet. She was not on a couch but in a roadside ditch strewn with sharp rocks and pebbles. Bayberry and other bushes covered the distance between her and a narrow dirt road.

"How did I get here?" Nancy asked herself, rubbing her eyes. Dimly she recalled the dream in which elves had transported her from her resting place on the cliff. Had someone actually carried her to the roadside?

"Either I wandered in my sleep, or I'm having hallucinations. Perhaps I struck my head in the cave."

Getting to her feet, Nancy gingerly tested her arms and legs. They were stiff and cramped, but she did not have a single scratch.

"Who knows, I may have been lying in that ditch for an hour or longer," she reasoned, not trusting the time on her water-soaked watch. "I wonder what Bess and George thought when I didn't show up. Probably they went home. I must find a phone and call them!"

Though confused by her experience, and frightened that another lapse of memory might overtake her, Nancy tramped quickly down the road. She kept hoping a car would pass, but none came along.

At length she reached a farmhouse. Seeing a well in the yard, she crossed a cinder path to draw herself a cool drink. A woman, wearing a faded gingham apron, peered curiously out the screen door.

"Goodness!" she exclaimed, coming outside. "You look all tuckered out! Have you walked far?"

Nancy hung up the long-handled dipper from which she had been drinking.

"Yes, I've walked a long distance," she said quietly. "My friends and I had an accident with our boat. May I use your phone?"

"Bless you, we haven't one. The nearest phone is at the Gladstone Dairy, half a mile down the road." Nancy looked so discouraged that the woman added kindly, "Do sit down and tell me what happened. Are your friends safe?"

"I think so. We became separated. Where am I now? Far from Candleton?"

The woman stared at the girl curiously. "Don't you know?"

Nancy shook her head, dropping into a chair near the kitchen door. "I'm a stranger here. After the accident, I became confused."

"You're about three miles from Candleton, and a quarter mile from the bay. You weren't by any

"How did I get here?" Nancy asked herself.

chance near Bald Head Cave when the accident occurred?" The woman's eyes opened wide.

Nancy could see that the farmer's wife was terrified of the cave. The young sleuth realized she must be careful of what she said.

"Is Bald Head Cave near here?" she countered innocently.

"Over there." The woman pointed in a south-easterly direction. "Fishing's good thereabouts," she added, "but you got to be careful. Once my husband was in his boat near the cave entrance when a flood o' water came rushing out. He was lucky to get away alive."

Bald Head Cave was a subject Nancy did not care to discuss any further. After declining the woman's offer of a glass of lemonade, she asked if there was anyone at the farmhouse who could drive her to Candleton.

"I'll pay him well," she added.

"Bless you, it's not a matter of money. My husband went to town and he isn't back yet. He'll likely drive in about sunset."

Nancy felt she could not wait. She thanked the woman for her kindness, then started off. Presently a car came speeding down the road toward her. It looked familiar.

"Why, that's my convertible!" she exclaimed.

As she shouted and waved the driver braked and the car came to a halt. At the steering wheel was Ned Nickerson, a friend of Nancy's, who was staying nearby to sell insurance to parents of two college friends. Bess and George were with him.

"Thank goodness you're safe, Nancy!" Ned cried, swinging open the car door and jumping out.

Bess and George also jumped out and rushed up to Nancy. "We were worried sick!" exclaimed Bess.

"We all had a narrow squeak," George said grimly.

Ned explained that he had stopped at Mrs. Chantrey's cottage. Learning from June that the girls had gone to Bald Head Cave, he had driven to the waterfront intending to rent a boat and find them. There he had met Bess and George.

Ned took Nancy's arm and led her toward the car.

"Has my father arrived?" she asked eagerly.

"Not yet." George shook her head.

"Any word from him?"

Again the answer was no.

"I'm sure your father is all right," Ned told them. "Maybe he sent a message that never reached you."

"I hadn't thought of that," Nancy conceded. She smiled at the young man beside her. "I'm sorry you found me looking so disheveled."

"Well," he said, laughing, "you look all right to me. But suppose you tell us about your experience after you left the cave."

Rather self-consciously Nancy related her strange dream and told of awakening in the roadside ditch. "I must have been completely out of my mind," she ended dismally.

"Perhaps you didn't wander in your sleep," Ned suggested. "You may have been carried."

"By elves? Oh, Ned!"

"By two man-sized elves. Notice anyone near the cave after the accident?"

"I wasn't in a state to observe anything." Nancy's blue eyes clouded with thought. "But I do recall—those voices—they sounded human!"

"Why do you suppose anyone would have carried you from the cliff?" George asked disbelievingly.

Nancy shrugged, declaring, "All I know is that when I investigate Bald Head Cave again, I'll go—"

"Alone!" Bess finished darkly. "So far as I'm concerned that mystery is welcome to remain forever unsolved."

Then, seeing a roadside stand, she reminded the others that they had not eaten since breakfast. After a quick meal, Ned again took the wheel.

During the rest of the ride to Candleton, the three girls exchanged accounts of their strange and terrifying experience inside the cave.

"Why don't I try my luck there tomorrow?" Ned proposed.

"Don't even think about it!" Bess said, and was vigorously supported by George. "The cave is too dangerous!"

When they reached Candleton, Ned picked up his car. Then Nancy, eager to learn if her father had written, suggested that they stop at the post office.

"Nothing for any of us," she reported in disappointment a few minutes later.

"Maybe there's word at the house," Bess suggested.

When they reached the cottage the young people heard the phone ringing. As they hurried up the steps, June came to the door.

"Phone for you," she told Nancy. "A gentleman."

"There!" Bess exclaimed triumphantly. "It's sure to be your father, Nancy!"

Nancy dashed into the hall.

"Hello, Dad?" she said eagerly.

But it was not her father who answered. The voice was that of a stranger.

"Listen carefully," he directed in clipped tones. "Your father requests that you meet him this afternoon at Fisher's Cove Hotel. Come as quickly as you can—alone."

"Who are you?" Nancy asked. "Why are you calling for my father?"

There was no answer. The man had hung up.

As Nancy turned slowly from the phone she found Ned standing behind her. After repeating the conversation, she asked for his advice.

"Don't go," he said instantly. "It's a trick."

"I'm afraid so myself, Ned. On the other hand, Dad may have a special reason for wanting me to meet him there. I must take a chance and go!"

"In that case I'll join you."

"The man's instructions were that I come alone."

"Why alone, Nancy?"

"I had no chance to ask any questions."

"If you insist upon going, I'll follow in my car."

While Nancy changed her clothing, Ned drove to the village to have her car's gas tank filled. By the time he returned to the house, she was ready.

Just as Nancy was about to drive away the phone rang again. This time George answered it.

"Hello?" inquired an agitated feminine voice at the other end of the line. "Has Nancy Drew started for Fisher's Cove yet?"

"Why, no, she's just leaving," George replied.

"Then stop her! Don't let her go!"

Before George could reply, the receiver clicked and the line went dead.

CHAPTER VI

Suspicious Actions

WITH mingled emotions, Nancy thought over the second telephone call. Common sense warned her she might be courting danger by driving to Fisher's Cove, but on the other hand, she was extremely anxious about her father.

"I'll carry out the first instructions, but I'll keep my wits about me," she decided. "If things look suspicious when I reach the hotel, I'll call the police."

After telling Bess and George to explain to their hostess what had happened, Nancy drove away. Ned kept close behind her in his own car. As they approached Fisher's Cove, however, he wisely put more distance between them.

Alone, Nancy parked near the front of a shabby, unpainted three-story building which bore the name Fisher's Cove Hotel.

"Dad never would have registered at such a

run-down hotel as this," she thought, hesitating.

Ned's car rounded the street corner. Reassured that she would not be alone, Nancy entered the building.

She walked up to the desk and asked the clerk for the number of Mr. Drew's room. The clerk was about to reply when a flashily dressed man appeared. He rudely interrupted with a complaint that he had reserved a large room with bath and had been given a small room with only running water.

Since Nancy did not wish to call attention to herself by protesting against the man's rudeness, she sat down and waited for the clerk to finish. To Nancy's relief, Ned soon sauntered into the lobby and seated himself on the opposite side of the stuffy room.

At that moment an elderly woman, with a mass of gray hair and wearing a flowered print dress, pushed close to her chair. As she passed, the stranger dropped a scrap of paper into Nancy's lap. Without speaking or giving any sign that she had noticed the girl, the woman walked on quickly, vanishing through a side exit.

Nancy glanced at the paper. It said, "Your father is not here. Leave at once before you get into trouble."

Nancy wondered what to do. She wished very much to show the message to Ned and ask his advice, but to speak to him would attract attention.

"This is the second time I've been warned," she thought. "I'd be crazy to walk blindly into a trap. I'll call Mrs. Chantrey and see if there's a message from Dad."

Since it seemed unwise to do this in the hotel, Nancy went down the street to a drugstore. Ned followed at a discreet distance. The call was discouraging. No word had come.

Upon returning to the hotel lobby, Nancy started toward the desk. Before she could speak to the clerk, a well-dressed man in a gray suit approached her.

"I am Dr. Warren." The man's manner was flawless, but the expression in his dark eyes disturbed Nancy. "Will you come with me, please?" Instantly the girl was on her guard, suspicious of a trick.

"Why should I?" she inquired, studying the man carefully.

"Your father is very ill upstairs."

"Oh!" The news stunned Nancy, but instantly she wondered if it were true. "Why hasn't he been taken to a hospital?" she asked.

"Your father did not want to be moved."

"Then you were the one who phoned me?"

"No, but I asked the manager to call you. He was leaving on a vacation trip and said that he would have someone else do it. Don't you trust me?"

The question caught Nancy unawares. She did not answer.

"Your silence indicates that you do not believe what I've told you," the man declared. "Suppose I have myself identified at the desk."

"Please," the girl said quickly.

The doctor took her by the arm, guiding her to the hotel desk.

The clerk, a tall, unpleasant-looking man with shifty eyes, was scanning the comic page of a newspaper.

"Hi, Doc!" he greeted the stranger, lowering his paper and staring almost insolently at Nancy.

"I wish you would tell this young lady who I am, Mr. Slocum," the physician said.

"Sure. You're Dr. Warren."

"Are you satisfied now?" the physician asked. Without giving Nancy an opportunity to question the clerk about her father, he steered her toward the stairway.

"Surely you're not afraid to come with me now?" he asked in an amused tone as she hung back.

The identification was hardly satisfactory, yet Nancy realized that if she accompanied Dr. Warren upstairs, Ned would know where she had gone.

Suddenly Nancy made up her mind that she was

being entirely too cautious. "Take me to my father at once!"

As she followed the doctor up the dusty, creaking stairs to a dingy third-floor hall, Nancy wondered if she might not be walking straight into danger.

"It's all so odd," she thought. "Those two calls! Then that strange woman who dropped the note into my lap! Who was she, and why did she tell me my father is not here?"

Nancy followed Dr. Warren down the dark hall. As he paused at a doorway, she could not hide her uneasiness.

"My dear, you really do distrust me," he said.

Nancy was ashamed of her misgivings. "It's only that so many strange things have occurred. For instance—"

"Yes?"

Nancy was still thinking about the woman in the flowered dress who had dropped the warning message into her lap. She decided not to tell him.

"Oh, nothing," she said.

"I'm puzzled about why you are so suspicious of me," said the doctor. Opening the door, he stood aside for Nancy to enter. "You are not walking into a trap," he added reassuringly.

Nancy smiled at him and without hesitation crossed the threshold. Her eyes focused on a walnut bed which had been pulled up near the windows of the small, stuffy room.

"Hello, Nancy," a weak but familiar voice greeted her.

She ran to the bedside and grasped her father's pale, limp hand. He looked so changed that his appearance shocked her.

"Dad!" she cried, stooping to kiss his cold, damp forehead. "Oh, what has happened to you?"

"So—glad—you—came, Nancy," he murmured.

He smiled at her, then closed his eyes as if asleep. Badly frightened, Nancy turned questioning eyes upon the doctor.

"Your father's case is most puzzling," he said in an undertone. "After he was found practically unconscious by one of the hotel maids, the manager called me here to examine him."

"How did my father come to this hotel, Doctor?" Nancy asked.

"By taxi, I was told. Apparently he was ill when he arrived. I questioned him, but he insisted that he did not wish to talk about it until you came."

"Why didn't someone get in touch with me sooner?" Nancy demanded.

The physician shrugged. "I wasn't called in until this afternoon," he replied. "When your father asked to see you, I inquired what the phone number was and asked the manager to contact you immediately."

"Has Dad been in this drowsy state ever since the maid found him?"

"Oh no. At times he rallies strongly, then has a relapse."

Mr. Drew's eyes fluttered open and he gazed steadily at Nancy as she knelt beside him.

"I must talk to you—alone," the lawyer said to his daughter.

Dr. Warren picked up his black bag from the dresser. "If you need me, I can be reached by phone at 424–3800," he told Nancy. "Your father may remain strong and able to talk for several hours. If he has another sinking spell, call me at once." Nancy nodded.

She asked how much they owed for his services and paid him. After the doctor had gone, Nancy returned to the bedside. To her alarm, her father tried to raise himself to a sitting position.

"No! No!" she chided, pushing him gently back on the pillows. "You must lie quiet."

"Nonsense!" he exclaimed impatiently. "I have something important to tell you. I must do it while I have the strength."

Nancy bent closer for his voice was almost inaudible. "You saw those men who cheated Mrs. Chantrey?"

"Yes. Then I took the plane. We landed at a small airport about ten miles up the shore."

"What happened after that?"

"Started here by taxi, intending to phone you to drive over and get me. A woman who couldn't get a cab rode with me."

"A woman?" Nancy inquired thoughtfully. "Can you describe her?"

"Stout—dark—not very talkative. Wore a big hat and large dark glasses. She left the cab at the outskirts of Fisher's Cove."

"Then where did you go?"

"Can't remember much after that. I became sleepy and must have dozed off. When I came to, I was in this bed. Some time later the doctor was called in. But this sickness is no mysterious malady."

"What do you mean, Dad?"

"I'm convinced I was drugged."

"Drugged! Not by the woman who rode with you in the taxi?"

"Probably by those two con artists I visited in New York. We had coffee together, and they may have given me a slow-acting sleeping powder. After I told them I intended to prosecute to the limit unless they returned Mrs. Chantrey's money, they left me alone for a while. When they returned they were very arrogant. I remember—"

"Wait!" Nancy interrupted the story. "I think someone is at the door."

CHAPTER VII

A Mysterious Malady

NANCY tiptoed across the room and quickly jerked open the door to the hall. No one was there, but she was positive someone had been eavesdropping.

When Nancy returned to her father's bedside, he insisted that he felt strong enough to ride to Mrs. Chantrey's home.

"I'm glad you're feeling better, but I doubt that the doctor would want you to get up so soon," Nancy said dubiously. "Why, you were practically unconscious when I arrived!"

"Just seeing you has helped me a lot, Nancy."

"Suppose I telephone Dr. Warren and ask his opinion?" Nancy suggested.

"All right, but do hurry. I've had enough of this place."

"I'll be back as fast as I can. Don't stir from your bed until I return."

"Just as you say." Her father grinned weakly.

Nancy hurried to the lobby. She was alarmed to see that Ned was no longer there. Quickly she called the doctor's office but there was no answer. As she left the booth, the hotel clerk motioned for her to come to the desk.

"You were asking about a Mr. Drew awhile ago?" he inquired.

"Yes. I found him in Room 301."

"But we have no one here by that name," said the clerk, looking at a registration card. "Room 301 is assigned to Mr. John Blake."

"May I see the card, please?"

Reluctantly the clerk handed it over. A John Blake had registered for Room 301. The handwriting was unfamiliar to Nancy.

"This isn't my father's signature!" she exclaimed. "Who brought him here?"

The clerk shrugged. "That I can't say. I wasn't on duty."

Nancy was convinced the man could not be trusted. Although certain that he must have seen Ned leave the lobby, she did not wish to endanger the young man and refrained from questioning the clerk further. Instead she paid the bill, which was far in excess of what it should have been but made no protest. Once more she tried without success to reach Dr. Warren by telephone. Failing, she went upstairs and tapped on the door of Room 301.

"It's Nancy," she called when Mr. Drew did not answer.

She rapped again and spoke her father's name in a louder voice. Alarmed because there was no reply she pushed open the door.

"Oh!" she cried in dismay.

Mr. Drew was not there! The bed was empty and had been remade.

Nancy rushed to the closet and jerked open the door. Only a row of empty hangers greeted her gaze. Her father's clothing and overnight bag had disappeared!

As Nancy glanced about the deserted room she felt weak. Where was her ill father?

"I shouldn't have left him alone—not even for a moment," she blamed herself.

Greatly frightened, and trying to decide what to do next, Nancy moved over to a window. Looking down into the street, she was astonished to see Ned pacing slowly back and forth.

Her first impulse was to call out, but she thought better of this, and merely tapped on the windowpane. Hearing the sound, Ned glanced upward. Nancy put her fingers to her lips and motioned for him to come up.

She waited anxiously at the door for Ned. Several minutes elapsed. Then she heard footsteps in the hallway and angry voices.

"Now listen!" argued a man who Nancy guessed

was the hotel clerk. "If you don't stop pounding on doors I'll have you thrown out! Understand?"

"Someone I'm looking for is in this hotel. I intend to find her."

At that moment Nancy opened the door and Ned rushed forward.

"Where is your father, Nancy? Is he all right?"

Nearly in tears, Nancy told him what had happened. The callous Mr. Slocum listened coldly, and openly displayed annoyance as she suggested that Mr. Drew might have wandered into an unoccupied room.

"Very unlikely," he said, trying to dismiss the matter. "In any case it's not our responsibility."

"You have a responsibility in helping me find my father, who is ill!" Nancy corrected him, her eyes flashing. "How many vacant rooms are on this floor?"

"I don't know without looking at my chart."

"Are vacant rooms always kept locked?"

"They should be."

"But are they?" Nancy persisted.

"Not always."

"Then my father easily could have wandered into one of them. We must search for him."

"There's no sense in it," Slocum argued angrily.

"Perhaps you prefer to have the police do the investigating?" Ned put in coldly.

The reference to police brought speedy results. The hotel clerk quickly produced his keys.

Beginning with the room directly across the hall, he tapped on doors and opened one after another.

"You see, it's a waste of time," Slocum grumbled. "Nobody here."

Nancy paid no attention. She had been examining faint footprints on the dusty floor of the hall and now paused before a door at the end of the corridor. "Is this room occupied?" she asked.

The clerk could not remember. Without waiting, Nancy tried the door and found it unlocked. The room was dark, with curtains drawn at the windows. On the bed lay a man fully dressed, and sound asleep.

With a cry of relief Nancy darted to her father's side. Her first attempts to awaken Mr. Drew brought no results.

Ned turned on a light while Nancy shook her father vigorously. His eyes opened, and he yawned as if awakening from a pleasant sleep.

"Dad, you must try to stay awake! How did you get into this room?"

With an effort the lawyer roused himself. "Are we ready to leave?" Then he turned over and went to sleep again.

Only after Nancy and Ned had tried for several minutes were they able to awaken Mr. Drew. He drank a glass of cold water, which seemed to revive him.

"Now tell me how you got in here," Nancy

urged again. "Did you dress yourself after I left?"

"Why, yes, I think so," he answered, trying hard to remember. "Then the girl came."

"What girl? You don't mean me?"

"No, the maid. She wanted to make the bed and clean the room. I sat down to wait, and that's all I remember until you woke me up."

"You don't know whether you walked in here by yourself or were carried?"

"Now who would move him?" cut in the hotel clerk.

"He was in 301," said Nancy.

"John Blake was in there. You said yourself you didn't recognize the signature on the registration card. Furthermore," Slocum added, turning to Mr. Drew, "you're all mixed up about the maid. The girls on this floor don't start work until just about now."

Mr. Drew gazed at the man with sudden dislike. "A dark-haired maid entered my room to change the bed. That happens to be a point about which I am very clear," he said in a cold voice.

"You can identify her, I suppose?" the clerk asked insolently.

"I can if I see her again. How many girls work here as maids?"

"Four come on duty at this hour. Three others work the night shift, but they're not here yet."

"Send the girls to me, please."

Slocum looked annoyed for a moment, then a

slightly sardonic grin played around the corners of his mouth. "Okay," he muttered.

A short time later four maids, who could not understand why they were being summoned, came into the bedroom. Mr. Drew asked each girl a few questions, then permitted her to leave. He had to admit he had never seen any of them before.

"Perhaps the woman who came to your room only posed as a maid," Nancy suggested after the last girl had gone.

Mr. Drew nodded. "Let's get away from here," he urged. "The sooner the better."

Nancy suggested that he should go to a hospital, but her father assured her he was feeling much better.

"I want to go on to Candleton," he said stubbornly. "If I can walk to the car, a few days on the beach will revive me completely."

Nancy and Ned finally agreed to take him to Mrs. Chantrey's house. Nancy said she would telephone Dr. Warren of the change in their plans and bring the car to the rear entrance of the hotel.

"Your bill is paid so we can slip away quietly," she declared. "Ned, will you stay with Dad?"

"I won't leave him a second," he promised. "Signal with two toots of the horn when you're ready with the car."

Nancy told Dr. Warren of her father's improved condition and their decision to leave. Within five minutes Nancy had her convertible waiting at the front of the hotel. Not until her father was safely seated in the car did she relax.

"I'll follow you closely in my car all the way to Candleton," Ned assured her, "and stay around till your dad's well again."

Mr. Drew actually seemed to improve during the ride. And after he was comfortably settled in a downstairs bedroom of Mrs. Chantrey's home, he insisted he felt as well as ever.

Nancy, fearful that he might have another unnatural sleeping spell, watched him closely throughout the night and the next day. She read to him, turned on the radio, and her friends brought him delicacies from Mrs. Chantrey's tearoom.

"You're making an invalid of me," the lawyer complained that evening. "I feel fine!"

The next morning, before anyone was out of bed, Mr. Drew dressed, slipped out of the house, and went for a long walk on the beach.

"Outwitted my keepers, didn't I?" he said with a chuckle upon his return. "Now I've had enough of this invalid nonsense. Haven't you young folks anything to do?"

"Why, Dad!" Nancy laughed in delight.

"Go swimming!" he commanded. "Take a motorboat ride. Just leave me alone to read a book. I'm entirely well, I assure you."

Satisfied that her father was his former self once more, Nancy joined her friends for a late-morning swim. The young people enjoyed an hour in White Cap Bay, then went back to the house to change clothes.

Mr. Drew was sipping a lemonade, deeply engrossed in a book. Nancy and Ned decided to take their lunch to a picnic area outside of Candleton. When they finally returned to town, Ned parked his car on the main street and the two young people walked along looking at the shops. They paused before the window of a novelty jewelry store.

Suddenly Nancy heard the familiar tinkle of a little bell. She turned her head quickly. Madame and her attractive cosmetic cart were coming up the street!

Looking in the direction of the cart, Ned observed Madame with interest. Her dark-skinned face was shaded by an elaborate flowered hat.

"Say, who is she?" he asked. "I've seen her before somewhere, but I don't recall her pushing a fancy cart!"

Madame, who was now opposite them, did not seem to recognize either of the young people. She quickly pushed her cart past them and hurried down the street. Or was she only pretending not to know them?

"Maybe you're acquainted with her friend?" Ned questioned Nancy suddenly, his eyes twinkling.

He gazed toward a stocky red-faced man who

had emerged from the shadow of a nearby doorway, and joined the woman at the next corner. Both glanced back toward the young people.

"No, I never saw him before," Nancy replied, but she knew she would not forget his face. It was cruel and calculating.

The stranger made no attempt to buy any of the French woman's cosmetics or perfumes. Apparently he was well acquainted with her, for they conversed freely. The man gestured angrily, and Ned and Nancy guessed he was trying to force the woman to agree to something against her will. Once Madame pointed toward the young people. Wrathfully the man pulled down her arm.

"What do you make of it?" Ned asked curiously.

Nancy had no answer. She continued to stare as Madame and her companion hurriedly walked away together and disappeared in the direction of the beach.

CHAPTER VIII

The Collector

Soon after Nancy and Ned returned to Mrs. Chantrey's, Ned said good-by. Early that evening, before their hostess came in, Bess and George went to the movies. Nancy and her father sat alone on the porch.

"It's wonderful to be here with you, Dad," Nancy said affectionately. "But I'm getting a bit restless. You hinted at my being able to help you on Mrs. Chantrey's case. You haven't given me my job yet."

"That's right, Nancy. But you must admit I was delayed in carrying on my own work. Thanks to you, though, I got out of that awful hotel. Now I can continue where I left off.

"A New York broker named Harry Tyrox," Mr. Drew went on grimly, "sold Mrs. Chantrey a lot of bad stock. He and his gang of sharp opera-

tors must be prosecuted. I'm afraid, though," the
lawyer added, "that Mrs. Chantrey will never get
her money back."

"Have you told her?" Nancy asked.

"No, but I think she suspects it. The job I had
for you, Nancy, concerns Mrs. Chantrey herself.
I'm afraid if someone doesn't bolster her morale,
she may break down."

"Oh!" Nancy exclaimed, then whispered, "Sh,
Dad, here she comes."

Mrs. Chantrey walked up the porch steps, looking very tired. Nancy asked about her day at the
Salsandee Shop, and she admitted she was having
trouble again with her employees. A waitress had
given up her job without notice, and one of the
shop's most reliable cooks had had an accident and
was unable to work.

"I don't know what I'll do." The tearoom
owner gave a deep sigh.

"Why not use me again?" Nancy volunteered.
"I'd love to help. I'm sure Bess and George would
too."

"It isn't fair to you girls," their hostess protested. "I invited you here for a vacation."

"And we're having a grand one!" Nancy declared. "Why, it's fun working at the Salsandee
Shop. And I have another reason for wanting to
be there," the girl added. "I'm especially interested in one of your customers."

"Do you mean the man who dropped the paper

telling about the XXX bell with the jewels in it?"
Mrs. Chantrey asked.

"That's right. Did he ever come to claim it?"

"No, he never returned. The paper is still in the
drawer at the shop."

Early the next morning Bess, George, and
Nancy donned uniforms and once more took up
their duties at the tearoom.

Nancy wondered if she would ever meet "the
bell man" again. She was very much pleased,
therefore, when she saw him come in at three
o'clock. He paused at the cashier's desk, and Nancy
heard him say in an agitated voice:

"My name is Hendrick—Amos Hendrick. Only
this morning I discovered the loss of a certain
paper. It's valuable, and I'll pay a good reward to
get it back. I'm not certain I lost it here, but
there's a chance it dropped from my pocket when
I paid my bill."

"I'll ask the owner, Mr. Hendrick," the cashier
replied.

"A. H., if you please," the man said firmly. "I
don't like to be called Hendrick."

There was no need for the cashier to ask Mrs.
Chantrey about the paper. Nancy identified the
man as the person who had sat at the table where
she had found the strange message.

"And you're the pretty little waitress who
served me so nicely," Mr. Hendrick said with a
smile.

Nancy searched the desk drawer where the envelope with the mysterious message had been placed. She went through its contents carefully. Satisfied that the paper was not there, she searched the other drawers. The secret message could not be found. Neither Mrs. Chantrey nor any of the employees was able to throw light on its disappearance.

Mr. Hendrick plainly was distressed. "That paper is very old and valuable," he declared.

Equally troubled by the loss, Nancy did not know what to say.

"Don't you remember the contents of the message?" she inquired.

" 'Course I do. That paper was found in my father's safe when he died and I know the contents by heart. But I don't want it to fall into the hands of a stranger!"

"Then you believe that some other person may be interested in searching for one of those XXX bells?"

A. H. gave her a quick, guarded look. George, who had joined the group with Bess, exclaimed impulsively, "You're making a mistake if you don't tell Nancy all about your paper and get her to help you! Why, she's solved more mysteries than you could count on your fingers and toes together!"

The man paused. His eyes sparkled as he said, "Ganging up on me, eh? You girls are three peas in a pod. Now why are you so interested in that paper?"

"Because we like adventure," Bess replied.

Mr. Hendrick's interest was aroused. He asked several questions about the detective work Nancy had done. She was uncertain whether he was joking or serious when he inquired:

"Well, how much will you charge to take my case? It's a tough one, I warn you."

"I solve mysteries for the fun of it," Nancy replied. "Suppose you tell me about your case, Mr. Hendrick."

"Not here."

"We might go for a walk along the beach. My friends and I have an hour off before the tearoom gets busy again."

"Fine," Mr. Hendrick agreed with enthusiasm. "Come along, all of you."

They walked a short distance down the shore, then the girls led the elderly man to a half-rotted log on which he could sit.

"To make a long story short, I've been interested in bells all my life," he began. "So was my father and his father before him. Know anything about bells?"

"Only that they ring." Bess giggled.

"No two ring alike. Some are high-pitched, some low, some have beautiful tone quality, and others are so harsh they insult your ears. Bells are with us from the cradle to the grave; they rejoice in our victories and toll our sorrows. They have enriched historical moments, colored romance, and struck terror in the hearts of the superstitious!

"My father was a bellmaker and so was my grandfather," A. H. resumed proudly. "They learned the art in Europe where they had their foundry. Know how to make a big bell?"

Nancy replied that she had only a vague idea.

"First you make a mold, and that takes a good many weeks if the bell is to be a perfect one. Then you pour in the hot, liquid metal. You have to be very careful. If the mold is not properly constructed, or you don't wait until the metal sets properly, the bell will crack when you take it out. A large bell must be cooled for a week or two before it can be removed."

"Tell us about American bells," Nancy urged, wishing to draw Mr. Hendrick into revealing more about the mystery.

"The first bell foundry in this country was established by the Hanks family, ancestors of Abraham Lincoln on his mother's side," Mr. Hendrick related. "Then there was Paul Revere. After the Revolution, he built a furnace in Boston and cast small bells. He also made large ones for churches. During his lifetime he cast nigh up to two hundred bells."

"What became of them?" Nancy asked.

"Ah! There lies the story. Fifty were destroyed by fire, one hangs in King's Chapel, Boston, but most of them are scattered over the country, and the folks that own 'em probably don't realize what a treasure they possess."

"Do you collect bells?" Bess inquired.

"Yes, I do. I've toured the country up and down looking for them. Own maybe fifty bells of all types and construction. I'm always searching for Paul Revere bells but right now I'm also hoping to locate another type."

"The XXX bell with embedded jewels?" Nancy asked softly.

A. H. nodded. "That paper I lost was found in my father's effects and was written by my grandfather. The bell was stolen from his foundry. I've spent eight years searching for that bell."

"And you haven't discovered any clues?" asked George.

"I found some, but nothing came of them. My search has been interesting, though. I've collected other valuable bells, and I've met a lot of nice folks. To get them to talk, I tell them about my hunt for Paul Revere bells. Then they usually show me all the bells on the premises, most of which are worthless."

"There's one bell I wonder if you have seen," Nancy said thoughtfully. "According to some people around here, it hangs somewhere deep within Bald Head Cave."

"Oh, I heard that story when I first came here," the man answered. "Nothing to it."

"Why do you say that?"

"Because I went there and looked around."

"And you didn't hear the bell?"

"No bell rang and no ghost appeared to warn me." A. H. chuckled. "It's just one of those superstitious tales."

"I can't understand why you didn't hear the bell," Nancy said, puzzled. "When my friends and I went there, we not only heard the warning bell, but we barely escaped with our lives."

Instantly Mr. Hendrick became curious, asking many questions.

"I must go there again!" he exclaimed. "Tomorrow, perhaps."

"Take us with you," Nancy suggested. "After our experience I'm sure you shouldn't go there alone."

A. H. chuckled. "I can't swim a stroke, I admit. Maybe I could use the help of three athletic girls if I should get in a tight spot with that ghost!"

Arrangements were made to meet him the following afternoon at a boat rental dock. The girls arrived ten minutes ahead of time. Amos Hendrick soon ambled along.

"I want it thoroughly understood before we start," Bess announced as she climbed into the boat, "that we're not setting foot inside the cave. It's too dangerous! We can hear the bell without going inside!"

"Agreed," said A. H. "But I warn you, if I

should hear a bell ringing, no telling what I'd do."

Nancy took the helm of the motorboat and they made a speedy trip to the foot of Bald Head Cliff. No fishermen were nearby, and the entire shore appeared to be deserted. Nancy idled the motor, allowing the boat to drift close to the shore.

"Don't go any nearer the cave," Bess warned.

A. H. said nothing, but from the way he smiled the girls knew he considered them overcautious. For half an hour Nancy kept the boat hovering near the cave entrance. Nothing happened.

"I'm getting tired of waiting," Mr. Hendrick complained. "Why don't we go ashore and——?"

He broke off, listening intently. Nancy and her friends also had heard the sound. Deep within the cave a bell tolled mournfully.

"You girls were right. There *is* a bell!" the old man cried excitedly. "A mighty good bell, too, with fine resonance and tone quality!"

Forgetting the girls' warning, he seized an oar and started paddling the motorboat into the cave.

"No! No!" exclaimed Nancy, grabbing his arm.

"Let me go!" A. H. insisted. "I must get that bell!"

CHAPTER IX

Cobweb Cottage

WITH a mighty jerk Nancy pulled the oar from Mr. Hendrick, pushed the throttle, and backed the boat away from the cave. A moment later a great flood of water rushed from the entrance. The boat was buffeted wildly by the waves.

"The ghost must have seen us!" Bess exclaimed dramatically, gripping the sides of the boat to keep from being tossed into the water.

Amos Hendrick, who had scoffed at the ghost tale earlier, was now trembling like a leaf. As Nancy steered the craft into less turbulent water, he said with an attempt at composure:

"This brings to mind a story told me as a child. According to it, a worker in a bell foundry near the ocean set sail in a small dory equipped with a tolling bell. It was said he joined some pirates who hid their loot in a cave. Nothing was ever heard about him again."

"Perhaps he was drowned at sea," Nancy remarked.

"So it was assumed, because for many years on moonlight nights other workers reported seeing his ghost walking on the water not far from the foundry."

"And you believe the story?" George asked.

"Many persons vouched for the tale. The ghost finally disappeared, and it was said he went back to the cave."

A. H. then added with a quick change back to the present, "I'd like to get my hands on that bell inside Bald Head Cave!"

"Please don't try," Nancy requested. "It's too dangerous."

"Let's go home," Bess proposed. "This place makes me feel uneasy."

"I have something I want to do first," said Nancy, staring speculatively at the cliff. "Who wants to go exploring?"

"I for one," George replied promptly.

Mr. Hendrick declined. "I haven't enough of the goat in me to climb around rocks. You girls go along. I'll stay and watch the boat."

Bess was glad of an excuse to avoid the expedition and remained with A. H.

"Don't let the ghost get you," George said jokingly as she and Nancy stripped off shoes and socks before wading ashore.

Soon the two girls reached the rocky beach.

There they put on their shoes again, and started up the cliff. Reaching the top they admired the view and waved to Bess and A. H. in the boat.

"I climbed up here a much easier way the day we nearly drowned in the cave," Nancy said. "Want to see where I had that remarkable dream?"

"So that's why we came," George needled.

"I'm curious to find out how the place looks, now that I have my wits about me."

Without difficulty Nancy spotted the general location where she had slept.

"I can't figure out how you reached the road from here," George commented. "If you walked in your sleep you were lucky you didn't fall off the cliff and kill yourself."

"I think so, too," Nancy said soberly.

The girls looked about, seeking a trail which would lead to the road. Suddenly George stumbled into a crevice between the rocks, severely twisting her ankle. Though she tried to walk, it was evident she could go no farther without great pain.

"I'll wait here," she decided. "You go on by yourself, Nancy."

Nancy hesitated, but George, who knew her friend wanted to do some exploring, would not permit her to give up the expedition.

Nancy went on alone, directing her steps toward a weather-beaten cottage nestled against high rocks. She did not recall seeing it the first

"Some tragedy must have occurred here!"
Nancy thought.

time she was on the cliff, probably because of the drowsy state she was in that day.

"What a lonesome place for anyone to live!" she reflected. "No trees. No garden. And it must be cold and windy in the winter."

Impulsively Nancy decided to call on the occupants. It was not until she was quite near the cottage that it suddenly occurred to her the men whose voices she had heard might live there.

But Nancy could not resist the temptation to investigate the house. It was so neglected looking that she decided the place was deserted. The curtains at the windows looked very soiled. A painted rocker stood on the porch, dust-covered and faded. It swayed gently to and fro in the wind.

Nancy went to the door and knocked several times. No one answered. Convinced that the house was vacant, she tried the door. Finding it had no lock, she lifted the latch and went inside.

What Nancy saw caused her to draw in her breath sharply. Chills raced down her spine.

A dining table which stood in the center of the room was set with two places. Food lay on the plates. But the food was moldy and covered with cobwebs. A chair stood precisely at each place, as though the occupants had gone away suddenly just before sitting down to the meal. "Some tragedy must have occurred here!" Nancy thought. "And not recently, either. The owners evidently left the cottage in a hurry and never returned. But why?"

The young detective peered into the other rooms and saw further evidence that the former tenants had fled quickly.

"It's strange they never came back to remove the furniture," she mused.

Deeply impressed, Nancy left quietly, carefully closing the outside door so that it would not bang back and forth in the wind. Reflecting upon the strange appearance of the house inside, she made her way slowly across the cliff. Midway to the spot where she had left George, Nancy was startled to hear a shout from below.

"That was Bess!" Nancy said to herself. "What has happened?"

She started to run. Out of breath and thoroughly frightened, Nancy reached the spot where George was standing.

"What is it?" she cried. "What's wrong?"

George answered by pointing toward the bay. The motorboat, with only A. H. aboard, was chugging off rapidly toward Candleton!

CHAPTER X

A Puzzling Disappearance

"WHAT's the matter with A. H.?" George cried furiously. "He can't go off and leave us stranded here!"

"Maybe he can't, but that's exactly what he's doing!" Nancy replied.

She cupped her hands and called to the elderly man. If he heard her, he gave no sign.

From some distance below, Bess also was shouting and waving. It seemed incredible that A. H. could not hear them.

"He's going off and leaving us on purpose!" George said bitterly.

Both girls knew that to be left alone on the cliff was a serious matter. There were no boats, and the nearest inhabited house was a long distance down the road. George, with an injured ankle, could not walk very far.

They watched, hopeful that the motorboat would turn and come back for them. Instead, it kept on steadily toward Candleton. Soon it was a mere speck on the water.

"There's only one thing to do," Nancy said. "I'll go for help."

"Where?"

"If necessary, to that house where I stopped the other day. Perhaps there's a cottage closer."

"Maybe I could walk." George gazed dubiously at her ankle, which had become badly swollen.

"You'd never make it, George. We'd better get you down to Bess. You can wait with her."

Nancy supported her friend as they made their way down the rocky hillside.

Bess was shocked by George's accident and as puzzled as the others by the sudden departure of A. H. She told Nancy and George that she had decided to take a walk along the shore to stretch, after being in the boat so long. Suddenly, to her horror, the elderly man sped off.

After telling Bess of the plan to go for help, Nancy overruled her offer to go along. "No, you stay with George," she urged.

The sun was still high overhead and beat down upon the rocks. As Nancy set off to bring help to her friends, she could not stifle a feeling of resentment toward Amos Hendrick. What had possessed the man to leave them stranded?

"He must have had some reason," she thought.

"I don't believe he would abandon us on purpose."

Nancy stopped short. She was facing the front of the deserted cottage. The door was flapping in the wind.

"That's funny!" she thought. "I know I latched that door."

A dark shadow flitted around the side of the cottage. Had someone left the house, or was the figure that of an animal?

"It must have been my imagination," Nancy decided. "But just to make certain, I'll walk over there and find out."

The weather-stained cottage was as abandoned looking as when she had seen it before. Again she knocked. Again no one appeared. Once more she pulled the door shut and tested the latch to be sure it would not open again.

Before leaving, Nancy hurriedly circled the house, but saw no one. Yet she was uneasy.

"The wind couldn't have opened the door," she reflected. "And that shadow—"

In a hurry to reach Candleton, Nancy did not want to waste time. Striking out in what she judged to be the right direction, she was relieved to come upon a path which led out to a dirt road. Quarter of a mile farther on Nancy reached the spot where she had awakened the other day.

"How in the world could I have wandered such a distance in my sleep?" she asked herself.

Before long, Nancy came to the same farmhouse she had stopped at before. This time a car stood outside, its engine running. A man, evidently the owner of the place, started off.

"Wait!" Nancy hailed him. He pulled up at the gate.

"Are you going to Candleton?" the young detective asked breathlessly.

"That's right."

"May I ride with you?"

"Sure. Hop in." The farmer dusted off the seat, then swung open the door.

As the car jounced over the rough road, Nancy told the driver what had happened, explaining that she meant to hire another boat and return to the cliff for her stranded companions.

"By the way, who lives in the cottage on the cliff?" she inquired, hoping to pick up some useful information.

"Why, nobody."

"I mean, who were the occupants before the cottage was abandoned?"

"Sorry, but I don't know. My wife and I came here only a few months ago. We don't get around much or see any of our neighbors. Too busy trying to make a living from our farm."

He soon reached Candleton, and at Nancy's request the farmer obligingly dropped her off at the waterfront. He would accept no payment for the ride, insisting that it had not inconvenienced him, and he had enjoyed talking with her.

Nancy hastened to the wharf where she had rented the motorboat. She saw that the craft in which A. H. had abandoned them had been returned. But where was he? The young detective asked the owner of the boat if he had seen Mr. Hendrick.

"Sure, he came in about an hour ago," the man replied.

"Did he leave any message or give any reason for going off in the boat and deserting my friends and me at Bald Head Cave?"

"Why, no! You mean to tell me he deliberately left you girls in that forsaken spot?"

"He certainly did. I came to town for help. My friends are still there on the rocks, one with an injured ankle."

"That was a mean trick. I can't understand it. Take the boat and go after your friends. Do you need any help?"

"No, I can manage alone. Thanks just the same."

The boat owner filled the fuel tank for Nancy, and to make certain she would be prepared for any emergency, gave her an extra can of fuel.

Although visibility was good on the water, late-afternoon shadows were beginning to darken the coast. At full speed, Nancy proceeded to Bald Head Cave, anxiously scanning the shoreline for a glimpse of her friends.

To her relief she saw a flash of color amid the

rocks at the base of the cliff. George and Bess were waiting for her on the beach.

Overjoyed to see her, they shouted and waved. Supported by Bess, George limped through the shallow water to climb aboard the boat.

"We thought you'd never get here." Bess sighed. "Did you see A. H. while you were in Candleton?"

Nancy shook her head.

"Just wait till I meet him again!" George said angrily. "I'll tell him a thing or two!"

"I still think he must have had a reason for deserting us the way he did," Nancy said. "How did you get along after I left?"

"Okay," replied George. "My ankle feels better now."

"No ghostly apparitions?"

"Not one."

"How about the bell inside the cave?"

"We didn't hear a sound," Bess said.

Without further delay the girls sped directly to the boat dock and drove to a doctor's office which Nancy had spotted on the main street.

The physician, a friendly, middle-aged man, examined George's ankle and bandaged it. "You have a slight sprain," he said. "Take it easy for a few days."

Nancy and the girls went on to Mrs. Chantrey's house. Mr. Drew, obviously upset, was walking restlessly about the lawn when they arrived.

Before Nancy could ask what was wrong, he noticed George's bandaged ankle and inquired what had happened. The girls told of their experience. Then Nancy said, "Dad, you seem upset. Tell us what's the matter."

"I'm disgusted. Read this!"

The lawyer thrust a telegram into his daughter's hand. It had been sent from New York and was from one of the young assistants in his office.

AS PER INSTRUCTIONS CALLED BROKERS OFFICE AND HOTEL. THEY HAVE SKIPPED. AWAIT FURTHER ORDERS.

"That's dreadful, Dad."

"Indeed it is! This ruins all my plans. The mistake I made was in giving Tyrox and the others a chance to make good. They should have been told nothing until I was ready to prosecute. Not only have they vanished with Mrs. Chantrey's money, but probably that of other investors as well!"

"You've never told me much about the case, Dad. What kind of stock was it Mrs. Chantrey bought? Anything I ever heard of?"

"The stock is not listed on any exchange. I do wish Mrs. Chantrey had asked my advice before she bought shares in a worthless perfume company."

"A perfume company?"

"Yes, a salesman showed her an impressive report of the firm's earnings, which of course was a fake. Mrs. Chantrey thought she was buying into an old, well-established company dealing with exclusive French products of high quality."

"What's the name of the firm, Dad?"

"The Mon Coeur Perfume Company."

Nancy stared at her father, scarcely believing him. Mr. Drew noted his daughter's startled expression.

"Don't tell me you know something about that company!" he exclaimed.

"I've seen the Mon Coeur products," Nancy replied. "There's a woman right here in Candleton who sells them. And I've seen a stout, red-faced man, whose looks I don't like, on the street with her!"

It was Mr. Drew's turn to stare.

"Your description of the man fits Harry Tyrox, one of the swindlers I'm after! He's the head of the company. Nancy, do you think you can find him for me?"

CHAPTER XI

The Chemist's Report

WHILE Nancy was telling her father everything she knew about Madame and her fancy cart of cosmetics, Ned drove up and joined the Drews. He listened in amazement to the story.

"Did that woman speak with a French accent?" Ned asked suddenly.

"Yes."

"And did she wear her black hair pulled back, and have a mole on her left cheek?"

"That's a very accurate description," Nancy agreed. "But I didn't know you were close enough to her to make such a minute observation when we saw her the other day."

"I wasn't!"

"Then don't keep us guessing. Where did you see her before?"

"At the hotel in Fisher's Cove. When I saw that woman with the cart here in Candleton I thought her face looked familiar. Ever since then

I've tried to remember where I'd seen her before."

"She may have recognized you, Ned. That would explain why she hurried away so fast. Where was she in the hotel?"

"She was coming down from the third floor as I was on my way up, and told me you had left the hotel. I didn't reveal that you had just signaled to me from the window. But she must have sent the clerk up after me. They didn't want me to find you and your father!"

"It looks as if you've hit upon a good clue to locate the Mon Coeur swindlers," Mr. Drew reflected. "Let's take the car and see if we can find the woman with the cart."

For an hour the three searched through Candleton, asking for Madame. No one had seen her for several days.

"She probably left town after she saw us, Ned," Nancy said. "Maybe she went back to Fisher's Cove."

"And you'd like to go there to find out," Ned remarked, smiling. "How about you both having dinner with me in Fisher's Cove?"

Mr. Drew declined, saying he expected a phone call from his young assistant who was in New York.

The three returned to the Chantrey house. While Nancy showered and changed her clothes, Ned chatted with Bess and George.

Later, as he and Nancy drove off, he asked, "Shall we eat along the way or wait until we get to Fisher's Cove?"

"To be truthful, I'm dreadfully hungry," Nancy confessed. "I haven't eaten for hours. There's an attractive place about five miles from here."

"I know the one you mean," Ned answered. "They have good music and we can dance. We'll stop there."

It was nearly nine o'clock when they finished eating. Ned and Nancy were reluctant to leave the pleasant atmosphere, but finally they went on to Fisher's Cove and parked near the old hotel.

"Don't get into another fuss with the clerk," Nancy teased her companion as they went inside.

The interview with Mr. Slocum, who was on duty, started badly. When Ned asked if a woman answering the description of Madame had registered there, the man was as uncommunicative as before.

"I don't know whom you're talking about," he retorted, "and furthermore, I don't care. All I ask is that you two quit bothering me."

"It should be of importance to you to know the kind of people who frequent your hotel," Ned said.

"You'd better watch what you say about this hotel!" the clerk cried out.

Ned bristled, but Nancy restrained him, saying,

"We're not accomplishing a thing this way. Let's go."

"Slocum knows more than he'll tell," said Ned as they walked away from the desk.

Nancy told him that she had another plan for getting the information, and they left the hotel. From a nearby telephone, she called her father and told him of Slocum's attitude.

"How about having a plainclothesman stake out the hotel to watch everyone who enters or leaves the place?"

"A good idea," Mr. Drew agreed. "In fact, since we don't know the woman's name, it seems about the only way to spot her. I'll arrange it."

Nancy was not too hopeful that the plan would bring results. She remarked to Ned on the way back to Candleton that if the Mon Coeur swindlers ever had made the Fisher's Cove Hotel their headquarters, they certainly could have moved out by this time.

"Isn't it possible Madame is peddling her products in other small towns around?" Ned speculated.

"Very possible. I mean to do some investigating."

"And I'll make a date with you right now to help!"

Nancy laughed. "But I want to start out soon after breakfast tomorrow."

"That's okay with me," Ned replied.

"There's no putting you off, I see." Nancy chuckled. "All right. Nine-thirty in the morning. First we'll attend church," she added, "then look for Amos Hendrick. He owes us an explanation for running off with the boat."

Ned arrived promptly and they set off. After the service they went to the boat rental docks and boarding houses to inquire about the man but did not find him. Then, in search of Madame, they drove to one seashore resort after another. No one had seen the woman in days.

"At least we're following her trail," Nancy said, refusing to be discouraged.

She paused in front of a drugstore window which prominently displayed Mon Coeur cosmetics and perfume. "This shop is open," Nancy said. "We ought to warn the druggist not to buy any more of the products."

"These may be better than the stuff Madame sells from her cart," Ned suggested. "It's possible she gets good perfume and dilutes it to make a high profit for herself."

"I hadn't thought of that. Suppose I buy some of these and have them analyzed by a chemist."

"Good idea," Ned replied. "I have a college friend not far from Candleton who will make the report for us, and we can depend on it being accurate."

Nancy purchased a lipstick, a box of powder, and a small vial of perfume. Later that afternoon

Ned took them to his friend, John Sander, who lived a few miles down the shore. Only two years out of Emerson College, which Ned now attended, the young man already had become well known as a chemist.

"John promises us a report by tomorrow night," Ned told Nancy upon his return. "I suggested that he bring it over to Candleton. He's going to get hold of Bill Malcome—you remember him. We'll make it a sixsome for the yacht club dance. Okay?"

"Sounds like fun." Nancy smiled. "I'm sure Bess and George would love it, too."

When the cousins heard about the date, they were pleased. Both knew Bill, who had escorted George to several parties in River Heights.

"I won't be able to dance with this ankle," said George, "but Bill likes talking better than dancing anyway, so we'll catch up on the news."

The following evening the girls had just finished dressing when their escorts arrived. Nancy ran downstairs ahead of the others to greet the boys. They were talking with Mr. Drew. Ned introduced John, who seemed to be a pleasant person.

"Did you bring the report?" Nancy asked him.

"I can give it to you in a few words," the chemist replied. "The sample of perfume proved to be mostly water."

"I thought so!" Nancy exclaimed.

"The face powder contained chalk—the common schoolroom variety—mixed with a little ordinary rice powder to give it texture. The lipstick contains a cheap substance, which really is dangerous to the skin."

"We must alert the druggist who has been carrying these products," Nancy declared. "I'll call him tomorrow morning." With a sigh, she added, "Wait until poor Bess hears this! She bought a bottle of that perfume."

Bess came downstairs at this moment and met the chemist. The truth of his findings was not easy for her to accept. She was ashamed that she had not followed Nancy and George's advice.

"I'd like to know what the perfume is like," Mr. Drew spoke up. "Would you mind getting your bottle, Bess?"

She hastened to her room and returned with the bottle. As Bess uncorked it, a strange, not too pleasant fragrance permeated the air.

"That dreadful stuff gets worse the longer it stands!" George declared.

"Why, how funny—" the lawyer started to say, then sank into a chair, staring into space. Alarmed, Nancy darted to his side.

"Dad!"

"I'm quite all right, my dear," her father said. "But that perfume—"

"Cork the bottle," George ordered her cousin.

"No, no, that's not necessary," said the lawyer.

"The perfume doesn't bother me. But I connect it with something unpleasant."

"In what way, Dad?" Nancy asked.

Mr. Drew seemed lost in thought for several seconds. Then suddenly he snapped his fingers.

"I have it! I remember now!" he cried excitedly. "The woman in the taxi with me! She used that same perfume!"

CHAPTER XII

The Candlemaker Helps

As the other young people went outside to get into the cars, Nancy and Ned lingered behind to talk further with Mr. Drew about the woman in the taxi.

"Are you sure she had on Mon Coeur perfume?" the young detective asked her father.

"Positive."

Nancy asked him to describe the woman again. The lawyer said he had not paid much attention to her, but recalled she was dark, had rather large features, and wore her hair so it covered a good part of her face.

"She could have been Madame," Nancy said excitely. "Dad, you thought those Mon Coeur men in New York might have given you a slow-acting drug. Perhaps Madame was their accomplice."

"You're probably right," her father agreed.

"Maybe," Nancy said, "you weren't drugged in New York but by the woman in the taxi."

"But how?"

"With the perfume."

"You mean the woman may have mixed that sweet-smelling perfume with something to drug me?"

"Yes."

At that moment an automobile horn began to toot and shouts of "Nancy! Ned!" reached their ears.

"You'd better go along," the lawyer urged. "I'll talk to you in the morning."

For several hours Nancy enjoyed the music and dancing at the Candleton Yacht Club. When the girls reached Mrs. Chantrey's, they tumbled into bed and awakened rather late the next morning. As Nancy came downstairs she heard her father phoning the airport.

"Are you going away?" she asked as he hung up.

"I must leave at once for New York, but I'll return as soon as I can," he promised. "My assistant picked up what may be an important clue."

"About the Mon Coeur people?"

"Yes, Nancy. I haven't time to explain the details. A neighbor is taking me to the airport. Will you pack a few things in my bag?"

"Then I'm to stay?"

"Yes, I talked with Mrs. Chantrey before she

left for the tearoom. She won't hear of you or your friends leaving. You're to remain and work on the case here. You don't mind?" he added, a twinkle in his eye.

"Maybe I'll have the whole thing solved by the time you return. And the mystery of the tolling bell, too," Nancy countered, hugging her father affectionately.

She ran upstairs to pack his bag, and a few minutes afterward he rode away. Bess and George were surprised to hear of Mr. Drew's departure.

"Let's hurry up and eat. We ought to get started," Nancy said suddenly.

"Started where?" Bess wanted to know.

"I want to talk to Mother Mathilda, the candle-maker Mrs. Chantrey told us about. She's supposed to know everything that has happened around here for the past sixty years."

Presently the three girls set off in Nancy's car for the old section of Candleton. Bess declared that riding down Whippoorwill Way among the quaint houses and shops was like stepping into another era.

Soon after passing a moss-covered stone church, the girls came to an old-fashioned dwelling of pounded oyster-shell brick. Attached to it at the rear was a fairly new stone addition.

"This is the place," Nancy announced. A wrought-iron sign read "Mathilda Greeley. Hand-poured, perfumed candles for sale."

She parked and they rang the doorbell. When no one came, the girls circled the building to investigate the rear. Nancy peered through the open doorway.

"This is where the candles are made!"

From the ceiling hung hundreds of gaily colored wax candles of many lengths and sizes.

"Doesn't it remind you of a rainbow?" Bess gasped in delight.

At the rear of the room, a bent-over woman with white hair stood with her back to the girls. She was stirring a kettle of hot, green wax.

Nancy tapped lightly on the door before crossing the threshold. At the sound, Mother Mathilda turned and nodded for them to walk in.

"We're staying with Mrs. Chantrey," Nancy explained, smiling. "She suggested we come here."

"Oh, yes, I've heard of you." The lady went on stirring. "Look around."

Nancy and her friends became aware of a faint but familiar odor. Nancy asked what it was.

"I have been making perfumed candles," Mother Mathilda replied, "but they are a failure. The entire lot is ruined! Not in thirty years have I had such a loss."

"Are they bayberry candles?" Bess asked, since the color of the liquid was green.

"Oh, no, my bayberry candles are the only ones which turned out well this week."

The candlemaker pointed to a rack of fragrant

tapers, explaining they had been made by cooking berries, skimming off the wax, refining it, and pouring it onto strings suspended from nails.

"Isn't that a rather unusual way of making candles?" Nancy asked. "I thought they were always made in molds, or else the wicks were dipped into hot wax."

"You're right. But years ago my family perfected the method of pouring the liquid onto the wick. When one layer hardens, we put on another coat. But I was the one who added the perfume," she announced proudly. "And never in the thirty years that I've been making scented candles have I had a failure until now."

Mother Mathilda explained that after she added a newly purchased perfume to her "batter," it neither held well to the wick, nor produced the desired fragrance.

Nancy noticed three large empty bottles on a shelf above the kettle. They bore the Mon Coeur trademark!

"Did you use the perfume from these bottles?" she asked.

"Yes. I bought them from a woman who claimed her products were superior to any other on the market. But why am I burdening you with my troubles! You came to buy candles, or to see how they are made."

"We do want to buy some of the bayberry variety," Nancy replied. "What really brought us here, though, is to ask you about that woman who sold you the perfume."

Mother Mathilda looked surprised. Then she said, "There is little to tell. The woman, a foreigner, came here and gave me samples of a lovely oil. It seemed exactly what I needed for my candles, so later I bought a large supply. But the perfume was inferior to the oil."

"What a shame!" George murmured. "That woman has sold worthless perfume all along the coast."

"Have you any idea where she is?" Nancy asked Mother Mathilda.

"No. I asked several of my neighbors, but no one knows."

"It won't be easy to trace her, I'm afraid," Nancy said, worried. "Once she cheats a person, she's wise enough not to return."

"It must have been only Madame's perfume that was of poor quality," the woman went on. "Mon Coeur products are of the best."

Nancy stared at her curiously. "Have you used them before?"

"No, but Monsieur who sold me stock in the company showed me testimonials signed by a dozen moving picture stars praising their products."

This statement stunned the three girls.

"You also bought Mon Coeur stock?" Nancy asked.

"Monsieur Pappier, president of the company, sold them to me himself. Oh, he's a fine, elegant gentleman!"

"Can you describe him?" Nancy asked.

"Monsieur is a stout man with plump apple-red cheeks. He wore a velvet jacket with braid. His voice sounded husky as if he had a sore throat."

"My father may know the man. The description fits a certain Harry Tyrox, wanted in New York for a similar sale of Mon Coeur stock."

"You think he is a fraud?"

"I am afraid he is, Mother Mathilda. Did anyone else in the neighborhood buy stock?"

"Oh, my yes! Maude Pullet, who lives a couple miles down the road. And Sara Belle Flossenger, the seamstress, took forty shares. Also the tailor, Sam Metts. They all bought stock the same day I did."

"What a day for Monsieur Pappier!" Nancy commented grimly. "I'm sorry to tell you that the stock he sold has no value."

"Oh, it can't be true! There must be some mistake! Almost all my life savings were given to that man!" The woman sank into a chair.

As Mother Mathilda wept softly, Nancy attempted to comfort her by saying Mr. Drew was trying to trace the swindlers.

"Nancy is working on the case, too," Bess spoke up. "I'm sure those awful men will be caught."

After some time the girls succeeded in cheering

the woman a little. They bought several dozen candles, and changed the subject of conversation.

"Who used to live in the cottage on the top of Bald Head Cliff?" Nancy asked the candlemaker.

"I guess you mean the Maguire place."

"Did they leave suddenly for some reason?" Nancy pursued the subject.

The question seemed to surprise Mother Mathilda. "Why, not unless you'd call going to their heavenly reward suddenlike," she commented. "Grandpa Maguire and his wife died. But so far as I know, the son and his wife are still there."

"The place is deserted."

"Then the report they moved away must be true," Mother Mathilda remarked.

"Did you know the Maguires well?"

"Very well. Grandpa was quite a character!" The elderly woman chuckled. "He had a flowing white beard that reached to his chest. And how he did like to spin yarns! He was a lookout years ago."

"Lookout?" Nancy questioned.

"Grandpa Maguire had a powerful telescope," Mother Mathilda explained, "and he'd sit on his porch, watching the sea for returning fishermen. Whenever he'd spy one, he'd scramble across those rocks nimble as a goat, and drive his horse to town to tell the women. Then they'd come down to the sea to meet their menfolks."

"What became of the telescope?" Nancy asked,

recalling the man who had gazed at them through one the first time she and her friends had gone to the cave.

"I don't know," the candlemaker replied.

Nancy was wondering whether the man on the cliff might have been using the Maguire telescope. She had not noticed it lying anywhere in the cottage.

As they rode home, Nancy discussed her idea with the girls. George thought the man with the telescope might have been Amos Hendrick.

"A. H. is a strange fellow," Bess declared. "I'll bet he knows the secret of that cottage."

"I agree," said George. "When he saw Nancy and me climb the cliff and head toward the deserted cottage he went away in the boat. Perhaps he thought that would distract us from our investigation. He might have been afraid we'd discover something he didn't want known."

"But he may have an enemy, too," Bess stated. "Who else would have stolen the paper he dropped in the tearoom?"

Nancy had to admit there was something to her friends' theories. She was determined to question Amos Hendrick about why he had abandoned the girls at the cave.

The elderly man, however, seemed to have vanished from Candleton. For the next hour the girls made exhaustive inquiries. No one had seen him. Finally the three friends gave up and went to the Salsandee Shop for lunch. Mrs. Chantrey, learning they were there, asked if the girls would go on an errand for her.

"I've just had a phone call from Maplecrest Farm," she said. "They were to bring me a crate of berries, but their truck has broken down. Will you pick it up for me?"

Nancy said they would be glad to drive there. She and her friends headed for Maplecrest Farm, about two miles out of town on the shore opposite the cliffs. As she sped along Nancy passed a parked car. No one was in it, but down by the water, a hundred yards away, two men stood talking. They were looking toward the water. Nancy recognized A. H. and told the other girls.

"Whom was he talking to?" Nancy wondered.

The man's companion looked familiar. It was not until Nancy drove into the farm lane a few minutes later that she suddenly thought she recognized the second man.

"He's the one I saw talking to Madame!" she declared.

"Really?" George exclaimed.

"I'm going to find out!" Nancy declared.

"How about the berries?" Bess asked.

"I'll get them first.

Nancy quickly accomplished the errand, then turned the car and raced out the lane to the highway.

CHAPTER XIII

The Runaway

WHEN Nancy reached the spot where she had seen the two men talking, no one was there and the car was gone.

"Look, Nancy!" exclaimed George, pointing toward a boat chugging slowly away from shore. "There's A. H.! He's going toward Candleton!"

"Let's try to catch him!" said Nancy. She accelerated and they sped along the road to the Salsandee Shop. The girls left the crate of berries at the kitchen door and hurried off again.

"Now where are we going?" Bess asked.

"I've a hunch that A. H. may have rented that boat from one of the fishermen," Nancy replied. "Let's go over to the wharves and find out."

Nancy made inquiries and learned that her hunch had been right. Mr. Hendrick had rented a dory only an hour before.

"What a surprise he's going to get when he sees us!" George laughed.

When A. H. reached the wharf, the girls expected him to try avoiding them, but the elderly man greeted them with a smile and said:

"Well, I'm glad to see you. That saves me a trip. I was going to call on you and offer my apologies, but I've been out of town. Just came back last night."

"We did expect to hear from you and learn why you took our boat and left us stranded on the cliff," Nancy told him.

Amos Hendrick hung his head. "I'm right sorry about that," he said. "The truth is, I suddenly remembered I had an appointment. I couldn't wait for you girls any longer."

"Was it with the same man you saw today?" Nancy shot at him.

The bell collector looked surprised and asked how she knew that. Nancy explained.

"Yes, he was the same man," A. H. answered. "The other time Mr. James didn't show up." A. H. leaned forward and whispered confidentially, "He has a bell I might buy."

"Oh!" Nancy exclaimed. Then she asked, "What does the man look like?"

"Oh, kind of red-faced. Has a stocky build and dark hair. Why?"

Nancy evaded the question. "I might want to

talk to him myself sometime about bells," she answered casually.

Inwardly she was very excited. The description of Mr. James definitely fitted the person with whom Madame had been talking! Was he Harry Tyrox alias Monsieur Pappier?

Mr. Hendrick started to move off, but Nancy was not through questioning him. She wanted to know about another matter also. She asked him when he had last driven to the cliff above Bald Head Cave.

"Cliff?" the man repeated. "I've never been up on those rocks. Nothing there worth going for that I know of."

"We thought we saw you up there looking through a telescope," said Bess.

"Not me. I don't own a telescope. Well, I must go now." He smiled. "Hope you've forgiven me for running off with the boat."

After he had left, Nancy mentioned her disappointment about the talk with Amos Hendrick. Either the man was hiding facts for reasons of his own, or else he was the victim of a hoax.

"Well, now what?" George queried.

"Let's call on the people who bought Mon Coeur stock from Monsieur Pappier."

Nancy had written down the names of the victims mentioned by Mother Mathilda. At least one of them might be able to give a clue to the whereabouts of the swindler. After learning from Mrs.

Chantrey where the people lived, the girls set off.

Their first stop was at Maude Pullet's home. The woman wept on hearing the news that she had been swindled. Sam Metts, white-faced and grim, told the girls that the loss of the money meant his son would be deprived of a college education. The little seamstress, Miss Flossenger, sadly admitted she had given Monsieur Pappier most of her life savings. At each place Nancy acquired the names and addresses of additional persons who had been cheated by Monsieur Pappier.

"This swindle is snowballing," she said excitedly to her friends. "Unless we can put a stop to it, there's no telling how many other people will lose their savings!"

Nancy kept hoping she might uncover a clue to the whereabouts of either Monsieur Pappier or Madame. But the people she interviewed had only one address to offer: the New York office, vacated a few days earlier.

Learning that several persons in the little country town of Branford had bought stock, Nancy drove there in the late afternoon with Bess and George. Interviews with two purchasers brought only the familiar story of the fantastic profits which had been glibly promised by Monsieur Pappier and a companion salesman.

Discouraged, Nancy was leading the way to her parked car when she noticed a girl standing on the opposite side of the street.

"Isn't that Minnie, the girl who bought some cosmetics from Madame?" she asked. "The one whose mother tried to have me arrested?"

"Yes!" George agreed. "Wow! What a costume!"

The girl's face was made up heavily. She wore a scarlet, sleeveless dress and several necklaces of various colors. High-heeled patent leather shoes fitted her badly. As the girl walked down the street, she kept turning her ankles every few steps.

"Let's talk to her," Nancy urged. "She really looks pathetic."

The three girls crossed the street.

"Hello," Nancy greeted Minnie with a friendly smile. "Aren't you a long way from home?"

"Not half far enough!" the girl retorted, tossing her head.

"You've run away?" Nancy guessed.

"I couldn't stand it on the farm another day. I've changed my name from Minnie to Marilyn Glaser, and I have a fine job!"

"In an office?" Bess inquired, wondering who would employ such a gaudily dressed person.

"No, as a model. I demonstrate Mon Coeur cosmetics for a weekly salary," Minnie went on proudly. "Madame is going to give me a bonus, too."

This information excited Nancy, but she was careful to keep her voice even as she asked, "Where do you give the demonstrations?"

"We'll have one tonight at nine o'clock in front of the Branford Hotel."

"Oh, not until tonight?"

"We never have our demonstrations until late," Minnie explained. "Madame says night light makes everyone look better." The girl giggled. "You ought to see me. I pretend to look awful, and then she fixes me up grand."

"I see," said Nancy, suppressing a smile. "Well, I wish you luck with your new work." Then she added casually, "I can see you like working for Madame."

"She's a fine woman!" Minnie replied. "She's promised to pay for these clothes, and she lets me have all the free perfume and cosmetics I want." Minnie teetered away on her high heels.

"Too bad we don't know her parents' address so we could notify them where the girl is!" George exclaimed.

"I'll try to persuade her to go home," Nancy said, "but not until after the demonstration tonight. Girls, do you realize Minnie may solve the mystery for us?"

"Will you notify the police to be on hand?" asked Bess.

"I may. How I wish Dad were here!"

"You have a date with Ned tonight," Bess said. "Why not talk it over with him?"

Nancy said she would. When Ned arrived at Mrs. Chantrey's house and heard the news, he smiled. "I'm sure I can handle Madame myself, and Minnie, too. There's bound to be a policeman not far away, if we want him to make any arrests."

Nancy was not completely satisfied. But she admitted to herself that the presence of the police might forewarn Madame or her accomplices.

She and Ned started off, and shortly before nine o'clock they reached the Branford Hotel and waited near the entrance. Soon Minnie appeared looking very unattractive in a black dress, her face pale, her lips colorless.

"She's certainly carrying out her part of the bargain," Nancy mused.

"By the way," Ned put in, "where is the cosmetic cart woman?" He glanced toward a clock in the square. "It's ten after nine now."

The seller of Mon Coeur products had not appeared. Even Minnie showed signs of increasing restlessness. She glanced uneasily up and down the street.

"I have a feeling Madame isn't going to show up!" Nancy commented presently, beginning to be fearful her plans would fall through.

"I have the same hunch," Ned remarked.

At nine thirty-five Minnie suddenly lost patience. With an angry exclamation she started away from the hotel, convinced that her employer would not appear. Nancy and Ned sauntered forward and intercepted her.

"Isn't there to be a demonstration?" Nancy inquired innocently.

"I can't give it alone!" the girl snapped. "And I haven't anything to sell. Oh, why didn't Madame show up?"

"Maybe you'll never see her again," suggested Ned.

"I will so! Something must have kept her. I'll go to her home."

"Do you know where Madame lives?" Nancy asked, her heart pounding with excitement.

In reply, Minnie took a paper from her purse and read the address aloud.

"We'll drive you there," Nancy offered.

CHAPTER XIV

A Threat

DURING the ride to the address where they hoped to find Madame, Minnie kept up a chatter which exhausted both Nancy and Ned. But when they drove up in front of an old, dark house, Minnie became silent.

"It looks as if it's deserted," Ned observed. "You two wait in the car while I find out."

He had been gone over ten minutes when he returned and shook his head.

"No one there?" Nancy asked.

"Only a caretaker. I saw a light in the basement. He has a room there. The owners have gone away for the summer."

"Madame hasn't gone away!" exclaimed Minnie. "I know better than that!"

"Madame is not the owner of the house," Ned corrected. "No such person has ever been here. Madame gave you a false address."

At first Minnie refused to believe the truth.

When it finally dawned upon her that she had been tricked, the girl burst into tears. She had no place to go, she declared. Her last dollar had been spent for clothes.

"We could drive you home," Nancy suggested.

"And have my family laugh at me?"

Because she had no choice, Minnie finally consented to being driven to her parents' farm. But as they neared the place, she became more and more fearful of the reception she would receive.

As the car stopped, the door of the farmhouse flew open and Minnie's parents rushed out to see who was in it. When they saw their daughter they cried out happily, and as she stepped from the car Mrs. Glaser took Minnie into her arms.

"Oh, my dear, don't ever go away again!" she sobbed.

Tears flowed freely down Minnie's cheeks, and suddenly she remembered Ned and Nancy.

"These—these people brought me home," she said. "You can thank them."

Mr. Glaser put out a gnarled hand, and his wife wiped her tears and said, "Please excuse me. I've been so upset these past few days I forgot my manners. Thank you kindly for bringing Minnie back." She did not recognize Nancy, who was glad of this.

Nancy and Ned left the Glaser family ecstatic in their reunion. As the couple rode toward Candleton, Nancy became very quiet.

"Worried about something?" Ned asked.

"Just disappointed. I had high hopes for solving part of the mystery tonight, but—"

"But instead, you aided a poor girl who needed help badly, and I admire you for it, Nancy."

After Ned dropped her off at Mrs. Chantrey's, Nancy continued to think about the strange puzzle. The next morning, however, Nancy was her usual cheerful self. With Bess and George she went to the Salsandee Shop early, and helped Mrs. Chantrey arrange garden flowers on the tables and prepare fruit before any of the regular employees arrived. When three of them called in sick, the girls volunteered to stay and help out.

Soon patrons began coming in for breakfast. The first customer to seat himself at one of Nancy's tables was a dwarflike man she had seen in the tearoom before. He gave his order in a gruff voice, then became absorbed in the morning paper.

As Nancy went back and forth from the kitchen, she kept stealing glances at the man. Where else had she seen him? To satisfy herself, she asked Mrs. Chantrey about him.

"I don't know his name," the tearoom owner replied. "He's a rather unfriendly customer. Never so much as says hello, although he comes here regularly. Evidently his wife is an invalid, for he always takes food for her when he leaves."

That night after the shop closed, Mrs. Chantrey

invited Nancy, Bess, and George to a concert. The cousins accepted, but Nancy begged off, saying she would rather stay at home because her father might telephone, or even return. June was out and it was very quiet at the house. Nancy picked up a book, but instead of reading it she sat lost in thought.

"Who *was* that man at the tearoom?" she asked herself over and over again.

Presently a car pulled up outside the house. Thinking her father might have arrived by taxi, Nancy ran to the porch. But she was wrong. A stocky man with a dark mustache and beard alighted, pulling his felt hat low over his eyes. Seeing the girl, he stopped abruptly in the shadows and asked gruffly:

"Are you Nancy Drew?"

"I am."

"Then you're to come with me."

"For what reason, please?" The man's manner had made Nancy suspicious.

"Your father needs you. He's in trouble."

"I think you're lying and I won't go with you!"

"Oh, you won't, eh?" the fellow growled, losing his temper. "Well, listen to me! You and that snooping father of yours! Mind your own business, or it'll be the worse for you both! Understand?"

The stranger advanced toward Nancy. Frightened, she ran into the house, slamming and locking the door. Turning off the lights, she stood behind the living-room draperies and watched the man from the window.

He started toward the door, but changed his mind. He hurried to his parked car and drove away.

Nancy picked up a flashlight and ran outside to look around. Tire tracks were plainly visible on the sandy road. As she examined the pattern, her roving light revealed a small bundle lying close by.

"Here's something of his!" she thought, picking it up. "This must have fallen from the car!"

Inside the house Nancy examined the package under a bright kitchen light. A crude sketch of three bells in a cluster had been penciled on the plain brown wrapping paper.

Puzzled, she unwrapped the bundle. Hundreds of labels bearing the Mon Coeur trademark fluttered to the table and floor.

"So that man was one of the Mon Coeur crowd!" Nancy thought excitedly. She stared at the sketch on the paper. "I wonder if they're going to change their design from hearts to bells."

The idea so intrigued Nancy she decided to phone her father. At that moment the doorbell rang. Startled, Nancy tiptoed to the hall and peered through the window. She could see no one and called out to ask who was there. It was Ned.

*"I think you're lying and I won't go
with you!"*

She let him in and briefed him on the strange man's visit and the package he had dropped.

"We must trail that man if we can!" she added. "But someone may be watching the house, so I'll slip out the back way and meet you over on the next street."

She hastily wrote a note to her friends telling them where she was going, then let herself out the rear door. By the time she reached the appointed spot, Ned was waiting in his car.

"This may be a futile chase," Nancy said breathlessly. "But I saw the man's car turn down this street after it left Mrs. Chantrey's."

"Notice the make?"

"No, it was too dark to see the car plainly."

"Then how can we trace it?"

Playing the beam of her flashlight along the roadway close to the curb, Nancy did not answer.

"What are you looking for?" Ned asked, puzzled, and got out of the car.

Nancy pointed to tire tracks plainly visible in the sandy road. She explained that they were the same pattern as those she had found in front of the Chantrey house after the man's car had pulled away.

"I noticed that the driver hugged the curb," she added, "so we may be able to trace him."

"It's worth trying," Ned agreed. "Let's go."

Nancy expected the trail might lead to a highway. To her surprise, the driver had selected a back street in the Candleton business district. This made it easy to follow him, for no other automobile had traveled on the same side of the street recently.

The tire tracks led to a small print shop in an alley. There the auto had turned in, apparently parked near a side entrance, then gone on.

Inside the building a light burned brightly. A man in a printer's apron could be seen working over one of the presses.

"It's ten thirty! That fellow must have a rush order to keep open so late." Ned observed.

Nancy suggested they talk to the printer and find out if he knew the suspect. The thud of a hand press deadened the sound of their footsteps as Nancy and Ned entered the cluttered little shop. Not until they shouted did the stooped figure whirl around to face them.

"Doggone it all!" he protested. "I wish folks wouldn't sneak up on me! Always think I'm about to be robbed. Anything I kin do for you?"

"We may want some stationery printed," Nancy said as an excuse for the interruption. "Would it be possible for you to do it soon?"

"Miss, I couldn't even touch it for six weeks! Why, I'm wallowin' up to my ears now in commercial orders. That's why I'm puttin' in extra time tonight—tryin' to get caught up."

"Do you do much label printing?" Nancy asked casually.

"Makes up about fifty percent of my business. Been doin' a lot o' work for the Mon Coeur people lately."

Nancy was careful not to show her elation at the information. "Oh, yes, I understand they're putting out another line, too. What's their new trademark? Is it three bells or—?"

She purposely hesitated, and the old man completed the sentence for her.

"You mean Sweet Chimes."

"Are you going to do the work for the firm?"

"No. I'm too rushed. Anyhow, that fast-talkin' foreigner, Monsieur Pappier, said he'd rather give the job to another printer who is closer to where the products are goin' to be made. Said it wouldn't pay him to have any more work done here."

"Where is the place?" Nancy asked, trying to conceal her excitement.

"Let me see. Yorktown! Or maybe it was York-ville. I remember it had a York in the name."

"Did Monsieur Pappier call on you tonight?"

"Yes, just before you came. This mornin' he picked up a package. He started talkin' about that Sweet Chimes idea, and he drew a sketch of the design on the wrappin' paper. Tonight he came back sayin' he couldn't find his package. He thought maybe he'd forgotten to take it, but I guess he lost it."

"I think I've seen Monsieur Pappier," Nancy said. "Does he have a mustache and beard?"

"No," the printer replied. "Must be somebody else you have in mind."

"Probably," said Nancy. "I'm sorry we kept you so long from your work. Good night."

Nancy was excited as she and Ned returned to his car.

"It must have been Harry Tyrox, alias Monsieur Pappier, who called on me!" she remarked. "He put on a mustache and beard for a disguise! And he didn't have a trace of a foreign accent!"

CHAPTER XV

Spanish Scheme

ALTHOUGH it was now after eleven o'clock, Nancy had no intention of abandoning the search for the swindler. Consulting a road map which Ned kept in the car, she discovered that a small city named Yorktown was about thirty miles away.

"Ned, I have a hunch that's where Monsieur Pappier went! Let's follow him!"

"All right, if you want to, Nancy. But it's a long drive. Won't the folks at home be worried about you?"

"I'll call Mrs. Chantrey and tell her our plans as soon as we reach Yorktown," Nancy declared.

Forty-five minutes later she and Ned entered the Yorktown Hotel. While Nancy phoned the Chantrey house, Ned checked with the clerk. Monsieur Pappier had not registered there that night, nor had anyone remotely answering his description, either with or without his disguise, been seen there. Ned also drew a blank on Tyrox and Mr. James.

"Let's try the motels," Nancy urged.

"Okay," Ned agreed.

They made the rounds, but learned nothing. Nancy had known the trip might end in failure, but even so, she was bitterly disappointed.

As she and Ned were walking away from the last motel, Nancy stopped at the adjoining restaurant where there was dancing. She went inside and spoke to the hatcheck girl. When she joined Ned her eyes were sparkling.

"Ned, I just learned something interesting! A Señora Sanchez who sells cosmetics has been in here tonight! She hasn't registered, but said she was coming back."

"We're not trailing a Spanish woman, Nancy, but a French lady."

"We may be now! Oh, I'll bet Madame and Monsieur change names and nationality whenever the police get warm on their trail."

"The police!" Ned exclaimed. "Let's give this information to them, and start for home."

Nancy agreed, so a stop was made at the Yorktown Police Headquarters. The desk sergeant assured the couple a close watch would be kept for both Tyrox, alias Monsieur Pappier and Mr. James, and the señora selling cosmetics.

When they reached Mrs. Chantrey's, lights

blazed in the house, indicating to Nancy that her friends had waited up. They greeted them with eager questions. Nancy and Ned related what had occurred in Candleton and at Yorktown.

"I'm sorry not to have a better report," Nancy said.

"But you learned a lot," Mrs. Chantrey assured her.

A few minutes later Ned said good night, and everyone wearily went off for a much-needed sleep.

It was early the next morning when Nancy was awakened by George who told her Mr. Drew had arrived from New York. Nancy dressed quickly, then ran downstairs to greet him with an affectionate kiss.

"Did you find out anything about those swindlers?" she asked eagerly.

"No," he reported in disgust. "Our leads were worthless. Not only Harry Tyrox, but all the rest of his gang have disappeared completely. I hate to give Mrs. Chantrey this bad news."

"Why not wait a few days?" Nancy suggested.

She told her father about her sleuthing activities since he had left, including the two times she had seen Tyrox; her suspicion that he was in Yorktown; Mother Mathilda's story which might lead to the arrest of the perfume seller, and what she had learned from the people in Candleton and Branford who had bought Mon Coeur stock.

Although Mr. Drew was shocked to hear about the number of investors in the area, he was delighted at his daughter's progress with the case. The lawyer decided to drive to Yorktown and learn what luck the police were having in tracing the phony señora. He set off in a rented car.

Left to themselves, Nancy, Bess and George decided to go for a swim. They rented a motorboat and went to Whistling Oyster Cove. After a delightful hour in the water, the three friends lay on their backs in the soft, warm sand. Suddenly Nancy sat bolt upright.

"Why didn't I think of that before!" she exclaimed, springing to her feet. "It may explain everything!"

"You might try doing a little explaining yourself," drawled George, tossing a pebble into the water. "What's cooking now in that clever brain of yours?"

"The best idea I've had in a week! Girls, you must go to Bald Head Cave at once!"

"Not inside," Bess objected. "As a matter of fact, I don't even want to go close to the entrance."

"It's approaching high tide now," Nancy declared excitedly. "I want to check out a theory of mine at the cave. You girls take me around to the ocean side of the cliff and drop me off where I can swim to shore. Then hurry back to the bay and anchor when you can see the cave entrance."

"And leave you alone on the cliff!" Bess retorted. "Nothing doing!"

"I'm not silly enough to risk my life," Nancy replied. "Please don't worry. But we mustn't delay or it will be too late to find out if my theory is correct."

"If Bess and I drop you off, what are your plans?" George asked.

"That depends upon what I find among the rocks on the ocean side. But please hurry. I have to make a search before high tide and you girls must get to your station as fast as possible."

"Your scheme sounds risky to me," George said. "But tell Bess and me what we're to do."

"You're to watch the mouth of the cave closely. If the bell tolls or water starts to rush out, note the exact time."

"What do you expect to discover?" Bess asked.

"I believe that as the tide comes in on the ocean side of the cliff, it may rush through a tunnel in the rocks and gush out the cave entrance."

"You mean before the tide is very high on the White Cap Bay side?" George asked.

"Yes. You recall that when we heard the bell toll, the tide had not turned in the bay."

"There may be something to it, Nancy," George agreed. "But what about the tolling bell?"

"I'll know more after I've made my investigation. Come on! The tide is starting to come in. There's no time to lose."

The girls hurried to the motorboat and in a short time rounded the cliff into the ocean.

"Be careful," Bess urged Nancy.

Nancy made a clean dive out of the boat, swam off, and easily reached the shore. Because the rocks were sharp, she put on her beach shoes which she had tied around her neck. Clinging tightly to precarious holds, she began to climb. By now the tide was coming in fast.

"The tunnel should be here somewhere," the young detective thought. "I'll have to work quickly to find it."

Nancy moved toward a pile of debris deposited by the incoming waves. She crossed this and went toward a definite opening in the rocks. Then suddenly she heard a shout.

Pausing, Nancy glanced toward a ledge where a fisherman was motioning frantically to her. His words sounded like "High tide!" but she did not catch the rest, because the wind was blowing away from her.

Nancy hesitated, then advanced again in her search for an opening amid the rocks.

"Quick!" the fisherman shouted. "Help!"

Now Nancy realized the man was in trouble. Approaching the ledge, she saw that his right leg was pinned beneath a large rock.

Unless the leg could be freed, Nancy knew, the man would drown in the incoming tide!

CHAPTER XVI

The Telescope Spy

As Nancy rushed to his side, the fisherman gasped, "I'm stuck! Loose boulder fell. Got to lift it— tide coming in!"

Nancy looked about for the boat, hoping to call to Bess and George for assistance. But the craft was too far away to signal it.

With a few quiet words Nancy tried to encourage the frantic man. Then she began to tug on the boulder. It moved slightly.

"If you can help me lift this," Nancy directed, "we'll have you free in no time. Together now— one, two, three—heave!"

The fisherman struggled to lift, but his position made it difficult for him to apply any leverage to the weight on his leg. As he strained, Nancy began to fear that he lacked the strength for the task.

The onrushing tide was already drenching them both. It would be only minutes before the ledge would be completely engulfed.

"Try again!" Nancy urged. "When we lift the boulder, pull your leg out."

With one last effort the fisherman was able to help Nancy raise the heavy stone, and managed to free himself.

"Hurry!" Nancy cried as she assisted him to his feet.

She took his hand and pulled him along over the ledge to the safety of higher ground. Both were breathless, and so shattered by the narrow escape that for a few moments they could not speak.

Then the fisherman said, "I'm mighty grateful you came along! You saved my life!"

"I'm glad I could help," Nancy replied modestly.

"Fishing is my business," the man began, after introducing himself as Steve Hopkins. "I know these ledges—except, of course, for that loose boulder that cost me a good rod and several worrisome minutes."

He smiled sheepishly, then turned to Nancy with a frown. "But you never should have been fooling around down there! More than one person's been drowned when the tide comes in!"

"I knew what I was doing," Nancy defended

her actions. "I came here searching for an opening in the rocks. I know about the cave with its tolling bell and rushing water. I thought I could find an explanation for them over here. The tide wouldn't have been in for at least ten minutes."

"I guess maybe that's so," the man admitted. "But around these here parts you never can tell what may happen. You say you were trying to find a hole in the rocks?"

Nancy explained her belief that strong waves, dashing through a small opening, might be responsible for the rush of water through the big cave.

"Could be," Hopkins agreed. "But I've lived in these parts for well onto sixty years. I've never heard tell of any such hole in the rocks."

"Did you ever see the ghost or hear the bell?" Nancy asked.

"I've never seen the ghost, and don't want to. But I've heard that mournful bell," Hopkins replied. "Folks figure that the spirit of the young man who joined the pirates comes back to prowl in that cave. They think the bell is the one he had on his dory."

"A boat with a bell on it might be caught somewhere in the cave," Nancy said thoughtfully. "Has anyone ever investigated to find out?"

"Folks hereabouts got too much common sense. Anyway, what good would it do for a body to go in there and fetch the bell? Long as it tolls a warning, it keeps a lot of people out of trouble."

Nancy talked a while longer with the fisherman, but soon was convinced he could contribute nothing to a solution of the baffling mystery. "I'd better go meet my friends on the bay side now," she said.

"I'll show you a safe path to it," Hopkins said. After thanking Nancy again for his rescue, he pointed out a well-worn trail which she followed without difficulty.

Reaching the beach, Nancy saw George and Bess waiting for her a hundred yards from shore. She knotted her shoes about her neck, then plunged in and swam out to the boat.

"What happened at the mouth of the cave?" Nancy asked as soon as she was in the boat. "Did the bell toll?"

"Exactly on the hour," George replied. "We didn't see the ghost, but the water did rush from the cave the same as before."

"Then I'm sure I'm right," Nancy said excitedly. "By the way, I was just going toward what looked like an opening in the rocks when a fisherman signaled me for help."

After relating her experience and her conversation with Steve Hopkins, Nancy said she thought it possible that an old, wrecked boat with a bell attached might be lodged somewhere deep within the cave.

"You mean when the water comes through, it

makes the bell ring?" Bess asked. "But, Nancy, how do you explain the ghost?"

"So far, I can't. Someone must be putting on a ghost act. But where does he come from and where does he go? Frankly, I can't guess what reason a person would have for hiding there or dressing up in white robes. The only way to solve the mystery is by thoroughly investigating the cave."

"Not today!" Bess said emphatically.

Nancy smiled as she turned to start the motor of the boat. "No, I promised Dad and Mrs. Chantrey I wouldn't venture in there even at low tide. But that promise certainly hinders me."

"It may save your life, though," declared George. "This is one mystery I feel we should leave unsolved!"

Nancy did not debate the matter. Her silence as the trio returned to Candleton told Bess and George more clearly than words that their detective friend did not have the slightest intention of abandoning the enigma of the tolling-bell cave.

Nancy had no opportunity to discuss the day's events with her father. On reaching the Chantrey cottage, she learned that he had sent word he planned to remain another day in Yorktown.

"That means he must have unearthed some interesting clues!" Nancy thought. "Perhaps the police have traced those swindlers we're after!"

At Nancy's suggestion the three girls spent the

evening at the Salsandee Shop, assisting their hostess. While George and Bess helped prepare Dandee Tarts, Nancy waited on tables, hoping she might see Amos Hendrick again. She regretted having forgotten to ask him where he was staying. But the man did not dine there that evening.

Among the customers she saw the same dwarf-like stranger who made a practice of taking food when he left. He ate rapidly, with a display of very bad table manners. When he finished, he ordered the usual package of food, then departed. Though Nancy questioned several of the waitresses, no one could tell her the man's name nor where he lived.

"I've certainly seen that man somewhere besides here," she remarked. "It wasn't in a theater, yet he seems unnatural, like someone acting a part."

"He reminds me of an elf," one of the waitresses said. "Only he has such mean, cruel eyes!"

"An elf!" exclaimed Nancy. "Why, that's it! I mean," she added hastily, "he does have that appearance."

The waitress' words had recalled to Nancy the strange dream she had experienced last week on the cliff above Bald Head Cave. In a flash she knew that the characters in her dream were not visionary but actual persons! Had she identified one of the elves?

"I didn't walk from the cliff by myself," Nancy

thought excitedly. "As Ned surmised, I was carried by two men. But why?"

Realizing that such a theory might sound fantastic to the others, she was careful to say nothing about it, not even to Bess or George. But she was determined to learn more about the stranger.

Hoping that he might lunch at the Salsandee Shop, she made a point of working there the next day. The man did not come, but to her delight, Amos Hendrick strolled into the tearoom.

"Well, well, my favorite waitress again!" He greeted her, then made a startling remark. "You bring a fellow bad luck, though!"

"How do you mean, Mr. Hendrick?"

"A. H., if you please," he corrected her. "Remember that man I was telling you about who was going to sell me a bell?"

"You mean the one you met on the other side of the bay—a Mr. James?"

"I haven't seen him since, and he was going to bring the bell for me to look at," A. H. reported. "Now I'm afraid maybe I'll never see him again, and I believe he has something I've been hunting for all over the country."

"Not the jeweled bell?" Nancy asked excitedly.

"Mr. James didn't tell me much, but I have a sneaking suspicion that it might be," Mr. Hendrick confided.

Nancy was startled at the information. She felt

certain that Mr. James, alias Harry Tyrox, had not obtained the jeweled bell by honest means. Perhaps he did not even have it, but knew where it was and was trying to get hold of it. This might account for his not contacting A. H. again.

"Unless the reason is that he has left this part of the country permanently," she thought.

Nancy hoped this was not so, and asked the bell collector to let her know the minute he heard from Mr. James. Then she inquired what kind of a tone the jeweled bell had.

"Oh, a very pleasant musical sound, almost like one in the middle register of a set of chimes."

"Then your lost bell couldn't possibly be the one in Bald Head Cave?"

"Oh, no, that one has a deep tolling sound." A. H.'s eyes brightened. "I'd give a lot to get my hands on it just the same," he declared, "but I value my life too much. Can't figure a way to keep from drowning, or you can bet your last dollar I'd be inside that cave this minute!"

"Perhaps I can help you," Nancy said.

While Mr. Hendrick listened with rapt attention, she told him of her theory that the cave was flooded for only a few hours each day, and that the period of danger could be clocked accurately.

"Say! Maybe I'll go there sometime!" the man exclaimed. "You really think it's safe?"

"I have an idea that if a person doesn't venture

into the cave after the tide has started to come in, he won't be trapped by the rushing water. I'll let you know later."

Because Mr. Hendrick was so pleased at the information she had given him, he talked more freely while he ate his lunch. As she served his dessert, he surprised her by saying:

"I've been thinking things over since I've been sitting here. I have a hunch that man James may be mixed up with the thief who has the jeweled bell."

"What makes you think that?" Nancy asked, trying not to show her eagerness to hear his answer.

"Didn't I tell you I traced it to a son of the original thief? His name is Grumper. He's an ornery little fellow—extraordinarily short. Haven't actually seen him, but I've been told he's around here."

"You think Grumper still has the bell after all these years? Wouldn't he have been tempted to sell it, or at least the jewels?"

"Not Grumper. He's a strange sort of man, not much concerned with money. They tell me chemistry is his main interest in life. He got into a jam with the company where he worked, and disappeared. I've good reason to think he's skulking around here somewhere."

"How did you learn Grumper had the bell?" Nancy asked curiously.

"From that note found in my father's posses-sions. You saw only part of the message."

Nancy would have asked Mr. Hendrick more questions, and found out his address, but just then another customer sat down at a nearby table. A. H. immediately became silent. He left the tearoom before the young detective had an opportunity to talk with him again.

Later that day she and Ned went to the boat dock with the intention of renting a motorboat to do some further exploring at Bald Head Cave. There they learned that Amos Hendrick had taken a boat and gone alone to the cave.

"He may get into trouble there!" Nancy said anxiously. "I should have warned him not to enter the cave until I've had a chance to prove my theory about the tides. If I'm wrong, he may drown!"

"Then we must go after him, and we've no time to lose!" Ned declared.

When he and Nancy reached the base of Bald Head Cliff in the motorboat, they could find no trace of A. H. Had he ventured into the cave?

"Say, who is that up there on the cliff?" Ned asked suddenly. He pointed to a figure seated on the high rocks, peering intently at the couple through a telescope. He was not Mr. Hendrick, as George had thought when she and her friends had seen a man on the cliff with a telescope.

"He certainly looks familiar, though," Nancy remarked. "Why is he watching us?"

Her attention was distracted by a flash of white near the cave entrance. Distinctly she saw a ghostly figure retreat into its dark interior. Within a few minutes a bell from within started to toll.

CHAPTER XVII

Important Identification

"THE warning!" Nancy exclaimed. "Oh, what if A. H. is inside the cave!"

"If he is," Ned said grimly, "we're too late to save him!"

Fearfully he and Nancy watched as water began to boil from the entrance. A box floated clear, but to their relief, no body or overturned boat was washed from the cave.

Convinced that A. H. could not have been drowned by the rushing water, Nancy sighed in relief.

"Let's climb the cliff," she suggested, "and talk to the man with the telescope. He may be able to answer a lot of questions about this place."

Ned anchored the boat, and the couple waded ashore. They climbed the rocks, using the path up which Nancy had gone before. But when they reached the top, the man had disappeared. They walked around a while, and peered into the cottage, but he did not return.

"Show me the place where you went to sleep that time," Ned suggested.

Nancy ran ahead, searching for the exact spot. When she thought she had located it, the young detective waited for Ned. Presently she began to feel dizzy. The blue sky above became misty, as if a film had dropped over her eyes. Vaguely she recalled that the same symptoms had overtaken her the first day she had visited the cliff.

"Ned!" she called in a weak voice. "Ned!"

He ran quickly toward her. One glance at Nancy's face told him something was seriously wrong.

"It's probably the climb," he said solicitously. "I'll carry you to the beach and you'll feel okay."

He lifted her from the ground and worked his way down the steep slope. By the time they reached the beach, Nancy seemed better.

"I don't know what came over me," she apologized, deeply embarrassed. "I've never had spells like this before!"

Ned insisted upon their going home at once so she could rest. But after he had left Mrs. Chantrey's, Nancy subjected herself to a severe athletic test. She raced up- and downstairs four times without pausing. George and Bess, who entered the house, stared at her in amazement.

"I'm not crazy!" Nancy said, laughing. "I'm

only trying to determine if I get fainting or dizzy spells after strenuous exertion."

"You could be a star athlete!' George retorted. "Why, you're not even breathing very hard."

"I feel fine!" Nancy laughed. "This test certainly proves I'm all right. But there was something queer about the way I nearly fainted today while on Bald Head Cliff! When I was up there I became very drowsy—almost as if I'd been drugged!"

"Have you any theory about it?" George asked.

"Do you suppose," Nancy said, "that some gas could have escaped from crevices in the rocks where I was standing?"

"Did you smell anything unusual?" Bess put in.

Nancy said she had not noted any strange odor other than a sweet one like that of the wild flowers on the cliff.

Later that afternoon, at Nancy's suggestion, the three girls called upon Mother Mathilda.

"I want to ask her if she knows anything about the cliff that might throw some light on my experience," she said.

To the disappointment of Nancy and her friends the woman could offer no explanation. So far as she knew, no gases or fumes had ever exuded from crevices in the rocks.

"I'm glad you dropped in," the elderly candle-maker said. "When you were here the other day, I forgot to tell you about Amy Maguire."

"You mean the daughter of the Maguires who lived on the cliff?" Nancy inquired.

"Yes. She was an adopted daughter. Amy turned out to be a wild one. As long as Grandpa Maguire was alive she behaved herself pretty well. After his passing, she made her Ma a heap o' trouble, running off to marry a no-good."

"Someone you know?"

"No, and I never did hear his name, nor what became of the couple. But I know her Ma was heartbroken, and her Pa took it kind of hard, too. They never mixed with other folks after that."

"What a shame!" Bess commented.

As the girls rose to leave, the woman timidly inquired if any progress had been made in tracing Monsieur Pappier, the Mon Coeur stock swindler.

Nancy assured her that Mr. Drew was working on the case. "We are hoping that both he and Madame will be caught within the next few days," she added.

"I hope," said Mother Mathilda, "that he's sent to jail for at least twenty years! And that she's punished, too! Will I get my money back, do you think, or will the scamps have spent it?"

"No one can tell that until the swindlers are caught. But let's hope you'll recover a good part of it."

Nancy's words cheered the woman. Grateful

to the girls for taking so much interest in her troubled affairs, she insisted upon presenting each of them with four delicately perfumed candles.

"I used good perfume this time, and the entire batch turned out perfectly," she declared proudly.

A little later, at the Chantrey home, Nancy learned from June Barber that during her absence she had received a telephone call from Yorktown. Knowing that it was from her father, she stayed indoors for the next hour, and as she had expected, he telephoned her again.

"Nancy, I've been trying to get you," he began in an excited voice. "Can you come to Yorktown right away?"

"Certainly, Dad," she replied.

"Good!" the lawyer declared. "The police are holding a woman who may be the seller of Mon Coeur perfume. You're needed to identify her."

"I'll come as fast as I can," Nancy promised.

She explained the purpose of her trip to George and Bess. Then she headed her convertible toward Yorktown, maintaining the maximum speed allowed. When Nancy reached the town, she went directly to police headquarters.

As she entered the building the young detective saw her father talking to the desk sergeant. Seeing her, Mr. Drew rushed across the room.

"I'm glad you're here, Nancy!" he exclaimed. "If you're able to identify the prisoner we may crack the case!"

"Where is the woman, Dad?"

"She's in a cell now. But you'll have to select her from a lineup. Think you can do it?"

"I'll try."

"The woman will not be wearing a costume, which may confuse you," Mr. Drew warned. "You'll be given only one chance to identify her. If you fail, she'll be released."

"If I've ever seen the woman before, I'll recognize her," Nancy said quietly. "Tell the police I'm ready."

CHAPTER XVIII

The Hidden Door

As Nancy, her father, and two police officers stood behind a screen, other policemen escorted five women across a small stage which was brilliantly lighted.

All were heavy-set, dark-complexioned, and wore street clothing. Blinking under the bright lights, they stared straight ahead.

Nancy gazed at each woman in turn. Then, without the slightest hesitation, she said, "The one in the center is the perfume seller. She is known to me only as Madame."

"Good!" Mr. Drew praised her. "That makes the identification positive."

After the prisoner had been led away, he told Nancy he previously had identified the same woman as the one who had accompanied him in the taxi to Fisher's Cove.

"The woman who drugged you!" Nancy cried out.

"I'm convinced of it. We'll place charges against her."

Nancy learned that Madame, who had been posing as a Spanish woman while in Yorktown, had been caught by the police as she sought to sell Sweet Chimes perfume to the proprietor of a beauty salon. She had denied knowing Mr. Drew or having anything to do with the Mon Coeur firm.

"She refuses to tell us anything about her confederates," the lawyer added. "Fortunately, a number of names and addresses were found in her pocketbook when it was searched. The police are checking them now."

As Nancy and her father stepped into the corridor, they came face to face with Madame, who was being taken to her cell by two policewomen. Seeing the girl, she suddenly halted and glared at her.

"Your meddling did it!" she cried furiously. "You're responsible for my being held here! But just wait until I get free! Just wait!"

Nancy made no reply, and the woman, still muttering threats, was led away.

"Madame speaks English without an accent," Mr. Drew observed. "The truth is, she hasn't a drop of foreign blood. She was born in New York City and her name is Martha Stott."

"Monsieur Pappier hasn't been found yet?"

"No, but the police are hard on his trail. They think he's in hiding around here, but I can't stay in Candleton to await his capture. I must fly back to River Heights tomorrow. Have an important case coming up in Federal Court."

"Oh!" murmured Nancy, unable to hide her disappointment. "Then that means we must leave the case entirely to the police."

"Not unless you've lost interest." He smiled and winked.

"Oh, Dad! You know how much solving the mystery means to me! I hope Tyrox and his pals are still around here."

"I hope so, too, Nancy. We're not letting it be known that Madame has been caught. In fact, we planted information that she went back to the vicinity of Candleton. I believe she and Harry Tyrox work hand in glove, and he'll trail her there. I'd like to have you stay at Candleton a few days longer to keep in touch with the situation."

The next morning Mr. Drew took an early plane for River Heights. He had barely left when Nancy asked Bess and George if they would go out to Bald Head Cliff with her again.

"And have you go to sleep?" Bess exclaimed. "I should say not! Anyway I promised Mrs. Chantrey I'd help her unpack a lot of gifts which arrived yesterday."

Nancy finally prevailed upon George to make the trip by promising to drive to the cliff and to keep away from the cave.

"But I thought you were supposed to stay around here to catch Harry Tyrox who is posing as Monsieur Pappier and Mr. James," George reminded her friend.

"I am. Dad and the police set a trap to get him back to Candleton to look up Madame, but they don't think Tyrox will come out of hiding until nightfall. Meanwhile, I'd like to work on the mystery of the tolling bell."

"How do you expect to accomplish that on top of the cliff?"

"I think there may be some connection between the ghost in the cave and the disappearance of the Maguires. Another thing. I've been giving a lot of thought to the queer dream I had while lying on the cliff. I've decided one of those little elves may have been Grumper—the very short man A. H. told me about. A. H. said he thought Grumper was around Candleton."

"And you believe he's the ghost and lives in the cave with a tolling bell and sends up fumes through the rocks!" Bess exclaimed. "Really, Nancy, I think this time you're going pretty far out with your ideas!"

"Maybe," the young detective conceded.

She refused to say more, but could not get the

strange happenings on the cliff out of her mind.

"The answer may lie in the Maguires' deserted home," she decided. "Anyway, I'm going to look for a clue there."

Nancy drove with George to the footpath which led to the cliff, and parked. The girls walked the rest of the way to the abandoned house, gazing about in all directions to find out if they had been seen. Apparently no one was nearby.

"This place does have a spooky look," George said uneasily as they went up to the door.

Nancy pushed it open. Everything appeared exactly as she had seen it before. The moldy, cobwebby food was on the dining-room table, and a dust-covered chair stood at each end.

"I never saw such thick cobwebs in all my life!" George muttered.

A worn Bible on a marble-topped table caught Nancy's attention. She blew off the dust, then slowly turned the pages until she came to the family birth and death records.

"This is what I had hoped to find!" she exclaimed, and pointed to a notation in ink. "Amy's marriage is recorded here. Oh!"

"Now what, Nancy?"

"Amy married a man named Ferdinand Slocum! Why, Slocum is the name of the hotel clerk at Fisher's Cove."

"But Slocum is a rather common name. He may not be the same person."

"True," Nancy acknowledged. "Let's see what else we can find."

The other records were of no interest to Nancy, but she did find among the pages of the Bible a letter which had been written by Amy to her parents. Obviously it was sent two years ago, soon after her runaway marriage. In the letter she disrespectfully referred to her mother and father as being far behind the times.

"Maybe I don't love Ferdie," she had written flippantly, "but he's a prominent hotelman and we'll have a lot of fun together. Ferdie is a man of the world. He's a big businessman, not like those boys at Candleton who only think about following the sea. I'll write again after Ferdie and I are settled in our own hotel."

"I'll bet they never were in any better one than the Fisher's Cove Hotel," George declared.

"This note explains a number of things about the Maguires that baffled me," Nancy said elatedly. "George, the pieces of our mystery puzzle are falling into place!"

"Find anything else of interest?" George asked.

"Yes, here's something!" Nancy exclaimed an instant later.

George, however, did not hear her, for she had made an important discovery of her own. "Nancy, look at these cobwebs on the table!" she exclaimed. "They're not attached to anything!"

"Not spun there, you mean?" Nancy stepped to the table to look. "You're right. Someone is using this cottage as a hideout!"

"But why would anyone go to so much work just to make this place look weird and abandoned?" George asked. "We ought to call the police!"

"I agree with you." Nancy spoke quietly as she stooped to pick up a torn sheet of paper from the floor.

"What's that?" her friend asked.

"Mr. Hendrick's torn note that was stolen from the Salsandee Shop!" Nancy replied.

George started to cross the room to see the paper. But as she took a step, a masculine voice directly behind the two girls said coldly:

"Don't make a move, either of you! Put up your hands and march straight ahead!"

At the command, Nancy did not turn around. As she slowly raised her hands, she saw in a dusty wall mirror the reflection of the dark-haired man who had given the terse order.

He was a small person of elfin appearance. Instantly she recognized him as the man who came frequently to the Salsandee Shop—one of the elves in her dream.

"Step lively and don't try to turn around," he snapped.

Perhaps the man held a weapon, but Nancy could see none in the mirror. She decided to take a chance. Whirling around, she swung her arm directly into his startled face, causing him to lose his balance. As he stumbled backward, Nancy gave him a push, and over he went! From his hand fell a telescope!

Instantly the two girls followed up their advantage. George plumped herself on the man's chest and held his arms. Nancy searched him but found no weapon.

"What was the idea of frightening us?" George demanded. "Are you the owner of this house?"

"No, but you have no right here!"

"Have *you?*" Nancy questioned.

"Yes!" was the surprising answer.

"Suppose you explain some things," Nancy demanded. "Who put moldy food in the dishes and covered them with cobwebs to make it appear the house was abandoned?"

The man looked frightened but refused to reply.

Nancy asked, "Are you Grumper? And where's your partner?"

"No, I'm not Grumper, but that's all you're going to find out."

"You're the one who helped carry me from the cliff!" Nancy accused him. "You and your friend put me to sleep with a gas which came up through crevices in the rocks!"

"Let me up!" the little fellow cried out in anguish. "You're crushing my chest!"

Nancy and George tied the man's ankles together with the belt from George's slacks, then released their hold. They stood him against the wall and placed themselves between him and the outside door.

"You haven't answered my questions," Nancy reminded the man as his shifty gaze darted about the room.

The captive muttered some unintelligible words. He leaned against the wall, his hands behind him. Suddenly, from far away, seemingly deep beneath the house, a gong sounded.

Nancy was startled. A sardonic grin spread over the elfin man's face.

"It was a signal!" Nancy thought instantly, observing his pleased expression. "He must have an accomplice somewhere!"

Recalling how the little man had many times bought food at the Salsandee Shop for his wife, Nancy concluded that was who his accomplice might be. Then, too, there was the possibility no wife existed, and that actually the food had been carried to another man.

"Perhaps he took it to that second elf I thought I saw in my dream!" she reasoned. "Grumper, I'll bet. If he's anywhere near here, then George and I had better be on our guard!"

Nancy was convinced that the man before her had managed to sound the warning gong by pressing a button or pulling a hidden cord. Even at this moment his accomplice might be coming to his aid!

The outside door behind Nancy creaked on its hinges. Frightened, she turned swiftly. A shadowy figure loomed large in the entrance.

Nancy laughed aloud in relief. Ned Nickerson stood there!

"Hello, Nancy, George. Are you girls safe?" he called anxiously. "Bess told me you came here. I was afraid—" He stopped short and stared at the girls' prisoner. "Who—?"

Briefly Nancy told him what had happened. The story was cut short by the sullen little man.

"It's a lie! You'll not take me to the police!" he shouted. "I won't leave this house!"

The elflike figure flayed out with his fists, losing his balance. As he went down, Nancy said:

"Ned, can you take this man to the State Police alone?"

"With one hand!"

"Then go as quickly as you can and come right back. George and I will stay here. I must find out more about this place!"

Ned was reluctant to leave the two girls.

"Don't worry," said Nancy. "If this man had an accomplice who heard that gong, he'd probably have been here by now."

"I guess that's right," said Ned.

He agreed to drive the prisoner to Candleton and return immediately.

"I'll hurry," he promised. "Don't take any risks while I'm gone."

He bound the man's hands behind him, released his feet, and ordered him to walk to the car. The captive had no choice as Ned prodded him from the rear.

George felt somewhat uneasy when she and Nancy were alone. As Ned and the prisoner disappeared, she glanced nervously about her.

"That gong—" she whispered to Nancy. "Don't you think it means someone else is here? Perhaps in the basement?"

"I'm sure our prisoner hoped so," said Nancy. "Let's see if we can find out how he sounded the warning."

She began to explore the wall inch by inch. The young detective found a thin cord, shorter than her little finger, not far from where the fishnets hung. As she pulled on it, a gong sounded far off.

"That's how he did it!" Nancy cried. "But where is the gong? It sounds so muffled—as if it were underground!"

Apparently the house had no basement, for the girls could find no steps or passageway leading downward. The only door seemed to be the one through which they had entered.

Puzzled, Nancy wondered how the elfin man had entered the house. Certainly not through the outside door. She recalled the sudden manner in which he had appeared and his terse order, "March straight ahead!"

"Why, to march straight ahead would mean I'd have to walk through a solid wall," she thought. "Or at least through those fishnets!"

Nancy stared speculatively at the wall, almost completely covered with old cord nets to which dried seaweed still clung. On a sudden inspiration she tore away a portion of the covering.

"What are you doing?" George asked curiously. "Look!"

Nancy had uncovered a door hidden behind the netting. George stared in amazement.

"The house must have a secret room or passageway!" she whispered. "We've found the entrance!"

Cautiously Nancy twisted the knob, making no sound. The door was not locked. Slowly it swung inward on its hinges. Leading down were stone steps into utter darkness.

CHAPTER XIX

Trapped!

"GEORGE," Nancy whispered, "do you have my flashlight?"

"Yes, but it's too dangerous for us to investigate below. Let's wait until Ned returns."

Nancy flashed on the light. It revealed that the stairs led down to a dark narrow tunnel beneath the old house.

"I'll go alone," said Nancy. "You stay here and wait for Ned."

"Aren't you taking too much of a chance?" George asked anxiously.

"I'm sure our prisoner has an accomplice," Nancy whispered. "And I'm also convinced there's some tie-in between the Mon Coeur gang and the little man we found here. If that gong was a warning, someone may be downstairs destroying valuable evidence right now."

Disregarding George's protests, Nancy beamed

the light ahead and slowly descended the narrow steps.

She moved deeper into the dark passageway below and her light could not be seen from the doorway. George waited with growing uneasiness. Finally she could not endure the suspense any longer.

"Nancy!" she called softly. No answer. "I'm going down!" she determined.

On the old buffet stood an antique candlestick with a half-burned candle. Beside it lay a packet of matches. George lighted the candle, and holding it before her, descended the steps.

Reaching the bottom of the stairs, she groped her way along the passageway until she glimpsed a closed door a short distance ahead. Again George called to Nancy, but there was no reply. Just then her light flickered violently and went out. George had no way to relight the candle. She chided herself for not bringing the matchbook.

As she was about to turn back, George suddenly became aware of footsteps. The tread seemed too heavy to be Nancy's!

George flattened herself into a deep niche in the wall. A figure and the dim rays of a flashlight passed close by her. Moments later a tall man was silhouetted in the doorway at the top of the stairs. He went through and closed the door behind him.

George stumbled up the stairway and tested

the door. Her worst fears were confirmed. It was locked! She and Nancy were prisoners underneath the cottage!

In desperation George kicked and pounded on the door, shouting to be released. There was no response.

"That man, whoever he is, has probably left the house," she thought. "Oh, I must find Nancy!"

Remembering the door in the passageway, George groped her way down again. At her touch the door moved inward.

George could see nothing, for the room was dark, but she did note a strange sweet scent. As she breathed deeply, a dizzy, giddy feeling took possession of her.

"Why, Nancy had these sensations just before she fell asleep on the cliff!" George recalled. "I'm being drugged!"

With all the strength she could muster, George pulled the door tightly shut. She felt so weak her limbs barely could carry her away. Through sheer will power she stumbled along the passageway and up the stairs to the locked door. Dropping to the floor, she pressed her face close to the crack underneath and sucked in great gulps of uncontaminated air.

At once George felt better. Then, as she realized how narrowly she had escaped being drugged, a feeling of panic for Nancy's safety came over her.

"I'll have to do something!" George thought desperately. "But what? Oh, why doesn't Ned come?"

At that moment Nancy was indeed in need of help. After leaving George, she had reached the closed door in the passageway and cautiously opened it.

A dim light burned overhead in the room, revealing a strange sight. Shelves along the walls were filled with bottles, vials, and flasks of colored liquid. There were large quantities of perfume, lipstick, and face powder.

"The cosmetic factory!" Nancy thought excitedly as she closed the door. Her gaze roved to a table on which lay scattered samples of both Mon Coeur and the newer Sweet Chimes labels. Hanging above the door was a gong.

At that instant Nancy became aware of men's low voices. Expecting them to come through the passageway door, she frantically sought a hiding place. Several wooden benches which stood against a wall offered the only possibility. Quickly she crawled underneath one.

Nancy had just hidden herself when she heard the voices again. To her alarm the sounds seemed to come from behind the very wall where she crouched!

One of the men said, "I'll go join Franz on watch, but you have your orders, Grumper! I arranged for that old fool Amos Hendrick to come to the cave. All you have to do is get his money, and if you're wise you'll keep him there until the tide comes in. Then send him out in his boat. After that, you race up the stairway and escape."

Crouching beneath the bench, Nancy was startled to hear a key turning and to see that close by, another bench was slowly moving inward! Evidently it was attached to a secret door which now was being opened by the approaching men.

A rush of cool air struck the young detective's face. As she remained motionless, the door with the bench opened wider and two men, one with a lighted lantern, tramped in. Nancy caught a quick glimpse of descending stone steps, and guessed that they led directly to the interior of the tolling-bell cave.

One of the men was exceptionally short with fuzzy red hair. He had an unpleasant expression. Nancy was certain he must be A. H.'s old enemy, Grumper. From her position she could not see the other man's face, but his stocky figure was like that of Harry Tyrox, alias Monsieur Pappier and Mr. James! He carried a lantern.

Nancy listened intently to their conversation. Suddenly she heard George's echoing shout from the passageway.

"Nancy! Nancy! Where are you?"

The two men stiffened.

"Get to work, Grumper!" the stocky one ordered in a whisper. "We have visitors. Franz must've tried to signal us. Something has happened to him!"

Grumper pulled a bottle of blue powder from one of the wall shelves, and with a little water he quickly mixed it into a solution. Dividing the liquid equally into two containers, he jammed one of them into a tiny niche in the stone ceiling and left the other standing uncovered on the floor.

"Now I'll take care of Hendrick!" he said.

"Good!" the other replied. "I'll go out through the cave and up to the cliff."

"But whatever happened to Franz may happen to you!"

"No one is going to interfere with my plans," the taller man declared emphatically.

He extinguished the overhead light. Nancy watched as the two slipped through the door by which they had entered and closed it behind them.

"I must follow and help A. H.," she decided.

But as Nancy crawled from beneath the bench, a sweet-smelling scent began to fill the room. She became light-headed.

"The drug!" she thought in panic. "Unless I get out of here quickly, I'll never make it!"

The door through which Nancy had entered seemed miles away from her. In her stupor she believed that her only escape was through the bench door the men had used. Could she move it?

Using all her strength, she tugged at the bench. It would not budge. Feeling so dizzy that she scarcely knew what she was doing, Nancy made another desperate attempt to turn the handle and yank the bench door forward.

"Oh, please open!" she whispered. "Please!"

Suddenly it moved inward. Nancy staggered through and closed the door. Then she collapsed on the stone steps.

It was several minutes before her head cleared enough for her to think. The flashlight had fallen from her hand. After groping about in the darkness, Nancy recovered it and focused the rays upon the dial of her wristwatch.

"Only ten minutes until the tide is due to turn!" she thought. "Where is Grumper? If he carries out his orders, Amos Hendrick will surely drown!"

Without considering her own safety, Nancy started to descend the steep stairway to the cave. When halfway down, she heard the tinkle of a beautiful, sweet-toned bell. Switching off the flashlight, she paused. Below she saw a flash of brilliant light.

Making no sound, Nancy swiftly went down the rest of the steps. She came to a passageway that veered to the right. As the young detective rounded the corner she saw a white-hooded figure standing on the ledge inside the cave. The ghost was swinging a small bell which gave a sweet, musical sound.

"Just as I thought!" Nancy told herself as she hugged the damp wall to keep from being seen. "This is the interior of the tolling-bell cave! And that ghost can be only one person—Grumper!"

As the bell swung back and forth, it gave off flashes of iridescent fire. Only priceless diamonds could provide such a rainbow of colors!

"The stolen Hendrick heirloom!" Nancy thought excitedly. But at the same time she realized that it could not be the tolling bell. "That has a much bigger, deeper sound!"

Suddenly she heard the splash of oars. Someone in a boat had ventured deep into the cavern. Was the person Amos Hendrick, or perhaps one of the Mon Coeur gang? Glancing nervously at her watch, Nancy waited.

At intervals, Grumper tinkled the bell. When the boat came quite close, he suddenly stripped off his ghost costume and flung it aside. Then, still clutching the precious bell, he crept forward.

Nancy now could see that the man in the boat was Amos Hendrick. Presently he tied up his craft and stepped onto the rocky ledge. As he did so he saw the half-crouched figure.

"Grumper!" he exclaimed. "So we meet at last!"

"Yes, you trailed me to Candleton, but it will do you no good!" the little man cried out.

"You're wrong," retorted A. H. His eyes gleamed as he looked at the bell. "I won't haggle over price, but you'll sell it to me or go to jail!"

Grumper chuckled evilly. "That's impossible. You couldn't get the police if you tried. It's too late! The hour of doom is upon you! The bell is mine! I will taste revenge for what your father did to my father!"

"Grumper, you're crazy! My family always treated your father with more respect and consideration than was his due. The truth is, he robbed my grandfather while working in his forge! Now give me the bell!"

"Neither of us will live to keep it," the elfin man retorted, backing away. "It will disappear, just as the ghost who has frightened folks away from this cave will vanish forever!"

"You're talking wild! Give me that bell or I'll take it from you. I have three times your strength, Grumper."

"You may seize the bell, but you'll drown! Any moment now the ocean will rush through this cave!"

Nancy, knowing that the threat was not an idle one, called frantically from the stone stairway:

"A. H.! A. H.! It's true! The tide will turn any minute! We must all get out of the cave before it's too late!"

The old man looked at the girl as if she were a ghost. "Nancy Drew! How did you get here?"

"Never mind! We're all in danger!" Nancy cried. "Follow me up these steps!"

Grumper snarled at the girl and barred the man's path.

"You'll have to fight me to get past here!" he chortled. "Anyway, it's too late! I can hear the water now!"

Hopping about gleefully, the crazed man swung the bell. A. H. pushed him aside and dashed for the steps. Grumper laughed wildly.

"The waters will swirl to the very top of the cave stairs!" He chuckled. "And the door to the lab locks itself from the outside."

"Quick, you fool!" Hendrick cried. "Give us the key!"

"I threw mine away! We'll all die here to-gether!"

Nancy and A. H. were frantic. Although escape seemed impossible, they started up the steps. Grumper trailed them, gloating over his enemy's predicament. When they reached the top, A. H. stood gasping for breath as Nancy turned to Grumper.

"Why don't you try to save yourself?" she urged, hoping that he might know some other way out of the cave. "Your boss didn't ask you to give up your own life."

"That guy who calls himself Monsieur Pappier

"We must get out before it's too late!"
Nancy called frantically.

and Mr. James and half a dozen other names will no longer be my boss." Grumper laughed mirthlessly. "His real name is Harry Tyrox, and he's a trickster and a cheat. Why, he even tried to steal my jeweled bell and sell it to Hendrick. When I found him out, he bargained with me to share the money I'd get for it. But I've outwitted him! I'll take the bell with me to the bottom of the sea!"

"So that's what upset you?" Nancy managed to speak soothingly as she tried desperately to gain their freedom. "You thought Tyrox intended to take the bell. Just lead us out of this trap and we'll have the police put that man behind bars."

"It's no use," Grumper replied in a calmer voice. "I have no key and the secret door is locked."

"Then we really are trapped here?" Nancy asked, losing heart for the first time.

"Yes, we're trapped. I'm sorry you have to go, too. When you first came to the cave I tried to frighten you away, and later that day I hoped to scare you with sleeping-gas fumes. But you wouldn't leave me alone, so you must suffer too."

At that instant in the cavern below they heard a faint, gurgling sound.

"The water is starting through," Grumper said. "In a moment it will come with a rush!"

In desperation Nancy pounded on the heavy

secret door, but succeeded only in bruising her fists.

"Help! Help!" she called weakly.

Then suddenly Nancy wondered if her mind was playing a cruel trick on her. From behind the door had she heard footsteps and a muffled voice?

CHAPTER XX

The Bell's Secret

FRANTICALLY Nancy pounded on the heavy door. Again she heard the muffled voice on the other side, but could not make out the words. Maybe the person was asking where the secret door was.

"The bench!" she cried. "Pull on the bench!"

At that moment the tolling of the bell reverberated throughout their rocky prison, followed by a thunderous roar as the surf from the ocean rushed into the cave. Drenched with spray, Nancy and the two men clung to the wall. As the noise subsided, they saw the swirling water rising toward their feet.

"Pull!" screamed Nancy, pounding on the door as hard as she could. "Turn the handle and pull the bench!"

An eternity seemed to pass as the water lapped closer. Then slowly the door began to open inward. Gas fumes poured out, but Nancy staggered forward, holding her breath. Behind her came Amos Hendrick. Grumper, paralyzed with fear, cowered on the steps below.

Nancy caught a glimpse of their rescuer, a young man in a gas mask which protected him from the fumes. He was Ned!

"Water coming!" she gasped. "Man still below!"

"Go on!" he shouted to Nancy.

She assisted Amos Hendrick to the passageway, where the air was comparatively fresh. Ned ran down to the frightened little man on the stairway and hustled him inside the laboratory. Barely in time to prevent the room from being flooded, Ned pushed the bench door shut.

Then he turned to Grumper. The man had collapsed on the floor, a victim of the fumes he had concocted!

Ned picked him up in a fireman's carry. When he staggered into the cottage with his burden, he pulled off his gas mask. Nancy's first question was:

"Where's George?"

"She went down to the outside cave entrance with a trooper," Ned replied. "Nancy, you owe your life to George," he said soberly.

"And to you!" Nancy said.

He waved aside the remark and continued, "When I delivered your prisoner to State Police Headquarters, I asked one of the troopers to return here with me. We couldn't find anyone inside the cottage. Then we shouted your names, and heard George pounding on the door hidden by the fishnets.

"George was convinced you were lying unconscious in the fume-filled room. Fortunately the trooper had a gas mask, a flashlight, and other equipment in his car. That's about all there is to tell, except that when I couldn't find you in the laboratory I became desperate. Just as I started away again I heard you pound on the bench door."

Nancy was too shaken to say much. At that moment George rushed into the cottage wild-eyed. Seeing Nancy, she flung her arms about her friend.

"Oh, you're safe!" she cried. "And I thought—"

Ned turned Grumper over to the state trooper. "Anyone else downstairs?" he asked.

"No," Nancy spoke up, "but did you catch his partner on the cliff?"

To a negative reply, Nancy said, "The worst criminal of all has escaped—Harry Tyrox, who also calls himself Monsieur Pappier and Mr. James. He must have seen you coming and decided his freedom meant more to him than Hendrick's money."

"Just give me a description of him and we'll pick him up," the police officer said confidently. "I'll notify headquarters over my car radio."

Nancy and her friends returned to Mrs. Chantrey's house. Within an hour they were informed that Harry Tyrox had been captured on the road while attempting to flee. Immediately Nancy telephoned her father to tell of the arrests.

"Good work, Nancy," he said proudly. "I knew you wouldn't need me to clear up the case."

The next morning Nancy and the others were given permission to talk to Grumper and Harry Tyrox. Soon the whole swindling operation was revealed. Based on information given by the two prisoners, New York police were alerted to pick up the man whom Mr. Drew had met when he went to see Tyrox.

Ferdinand Slocum, the hotel clerk in Fisher's Cove, had been brought in for questioning. Frightened, the man admitted his part in the swindle.

"Harry Tyrox and I were friends. He offered me a cut in the cosmetic and perfume business if I would let him use the hotel for some of his shady deals," he confessed. "After Harry saw Mr. Drew in New York, he phoned me that the lawyer was coming to Candleton and something had to be done to keep him at Fisher's Cove. So I told Amy we had to get busy."

"Your wife?" Nancy asked.

"Yes."

"Go on with your story."

"I might as well tell it from the beginning. Soon

after we were married, Amy mentioned the hidden door and the passageway to the cave. Her foster father had a workshop down there."

"Surely he didn't build the tunnel himself."

"No, it was there when the Maguires bought the cottage. Old Grandpa Maguire discovered the closed-up entranceway one day when he was repairing the wall, and the secret was always kept in the family. The cave originally was used as a hideout by pirates."

"Tell me about the cosmetic factory," Nancy urged. "Whose idea was that?"

"Harry's. I foolishly told him about the workshop above the cave, and right away he thought he saw a chance for big money. The plan was to make cheap imitations of very expensive products and sell them under the Mon Coeur name. First, he got the Maguires out by telling them Amy was in trouble with the police and they would be disgraced when the townspeople heard about it. They packed up and moved away immediately."

"How did Grumper figure in the scheme?"

"Harry knew about him and some crimes he'd committed. He promised Grumper a lot of money if he'd come in with us and work as our chemist. Grumper thought he could use the money to go away some place where no one knew him, so he agreed. But he didn't figure on Amos Hendrick."

"He upset Grumper's plans?" Nancy inquired with a smile.

"He turned them upside down. Grumper was in a panic that Hendrick would find him and reclaim the stolen jeweled bell."

"How did he learn Mr. Hendrick was in Candleton?"

"Through his cousin Franz, who served as a lookout at the cliff. Whenever people came near the cave, he sounded the gong and Grumper, hearing it in the laboratory, hurried down and tried to scare them away with his ghost act."

"Then the rush of water and the tolling bell had nothing to do with his appearances," said Nancy.

"No, but they sometimes happened close together," Slocum replied. "Whenever Franz spied someone on the cliff, he would run down to the laboratory and have Grumper send up sleeping-gas fumes through crevices in the rocks."

"I know now that Franz was the second little elf I thought I saw in my dream!" Nancy exclaimed. "He frequently came to the Salsandee Shop and carried away food."

"Yes, he had a little car hidden in some bushes at the foot of the cliff."

"I suppose he also stole the note A. H. lost at the shop," Nancy said.

"That's right. Franz knew A. H. by sight and happened to see him drop the note in the tearoom. Later he stole it from the drawer. Before Franz could show it to Grumper, Harry Tyrox got hold of it and then the cat was out of the bag. He tried to get the bell, but Grumper wouldn't let him have it. Harry was afraid of him because he could put people to sleep with his drugs."

"Tell me," said Nancy, "were you the person who passed my friend George in the passageway yesterday morning?"

Slocum started. "I was there but I didn't know anybody else was. We have a secret closet with a stone door, where we keep Mon Coeur products. I was in the closet. When I came out the passage was dark. My flashlight didn't show up anybody."

"Did you lock the door at the top of the stairs?"

"Yes."

Nancy went on, "You haven't told me how my father was drugged."

"When your father told Harry and his pal he intended to prosecute, Harry knew we had to do something quick. Harry followed Mr. Drew to the New York airport, then telephoned Madame to intercept him. We were ordered to see that he conveniently disappeared for a few weeks. Grumper made up a vial of liquid which would turn into sleeping fumes, and gave it to Madame. She arranged to get into a taxi with Mr. Drew, and just before leaving it, opened the bottle and dropped a small amount of the liquid on his coat. It was just enough to affect him but not the driver."

"How did my father reach Fisher's Cove Hotel?"

"The driver of the cab had been paid by our men and knew what to do. He took your father there. I registered him under another name, and then kept an eye on him."

"It was Madame, I·suppose, disguised as a maid, who had my father moved from his room."

"Right. Whenever he was getting better, she gave him another dose and put him to sleep.

"By accident the hotel manager discovered your father's condition and called Dr. Warren. When Harry overheard the manager tell me to call you, he decided that you were to be drugged too and removed with your father to some other hideout. But Amy, my wife, was afraid I was getting in too deep with the gang and wanted to spike that part of the plan. That's why she warned you by telephone to keep away. At the last minute Harry concluded the double kidnapping was too risky and called it off."

"Your wife was far wiser than you, Mr. Slocum."

"I wish now I had listened to her," the hotel clerk said miserably. "My wife works in a beauty salon. The day you came for your father she borrowed a wig from there, dressed as an old lady, and looked for you in the lobby."

"Then she was the one who dropped the note into my lap!"

"That's right."

Nancy and her friends were happy when they learned that Harry Tyrox, alias Monsieur Pappier and Mr. James, together with his New York accomplice, still possessed most of the money he had fleeced from innocent victims. Mrs. Chantrey, Mother Mathilda, and the others who had bought the worthless stock would recover a sizable amount of the cash they had put into it.

"What will become of Amy?" George asked, as the girls sat on the Chantrey porch after lunch discussing the case. "Her husband will be sentenced to prison, and she'll be left alone."

"The Maguires are taking her back," Nancy replied. "Mother Mathilda phoned me a little while ago. They're all returning to the cottage in a few days—which reminds me, we should go there this minute!"

"But why?" Bess asked in surprise. "All the gang have been caught."

"True, but the mystery of the cave is only half solved. Mr. Hendrick recovered the jeweled bell from Grumper. But we know it wasn't his bell that frightened people away from the place. Another bell must be somewhere in the cave. I intend to find out!" Nancy sprang to her feet. "Anyone going with me?"

"How about me?" inquired a voice from the driveway.

Turning quickly, the girls saw Ned Nickerson approaching the porch. It was his last day in Candleton, and Bess and George generously declined an invitation to ride with the couple to the Maguire home.

"Why this trip?" Ned asked. "Anything special?"

"I want to clear away the moldy food and cobwebs Tyrox and his men left there. The Maguires would be shocked. And I'd like to find the tolling bell."

At the deserted cottage the two spent an hour cleaning away the debris. Then Nancy looked at her watch. "The tide won't come in for a while. We can make a complete investigation of the cave."

Ned chuckled. "I came prepared! I have a gasoline lantern in the car, and it gives off a brilliant light. We'll really be able to see what's down there."

He went for it and Nancy found two blocks of wood to prop open the secret doors.

The cosmetic factory bore only a faint trace of fumes. Passing through it quickly, Nancy and Ned went down the stone steps to the bottom of the cave. With the tide out, it was possible to walk on the ledge to the entrance.

Nancy turned the other way, however, and asked Ned to focus the light in that direction. Almost at once she found the gaping hole through which the water rushed in at high tide. To Ned's astonishment, she reached her arm far back into the gap.

"What are you looking for?" he demanded.

Nancy did not answer, but a moment later she asked his help to pull out a rusty, corroded bell. As it swung slowly, a doleful tolling echoed in the cave.

"The warning bell!" Ned exclaimed. "How did you know it was hidden back there?"

"I didn't, but I got to thinking about the story of the pirates and the loot they hid here."

"Yes, but the bell never rang until recently," Ned protested. "How can you explain that?"

"My guess is that at the time the pirates hid their loot in this cave, the opening was very small and only a little water trickled through when the tide came in. Perhaps they placed the bell where it would be tapped lightly when water struck it, and they'd know the tide had changed.

"But as the years went on, the waves carved a wider opening, and more and more water poured into the cave. And just recently the violent action of the waves has caused the bell to toll loudly enough to be heard outside the cave."

"That bell must be very old," Ned commented. "Maybe it has been in this cave since Revolutionary War years."

"I'm sure of it, Ned." Nancy peered at the trademark, then excitedly she said, "This is a

Paul Revere bell! Just what A. H. said he was looking for! I should like to keep it. A. H. said yesterday he wanted to reward me for recovering the jeweled bell. This bell is reward enough for me."

"No one could dispute your claim to it but the pirates!" Ned chuckled as he took the bell. He carried it up the stone stairway, through the laboratory, and up to the cottage.

"It must have been very exciting in the old days," Nancy said wistfully. "How I wish I could have been here to solve a mystery when the cave was a pirates' hideout!"

"Mysteries!" Ned exclaimed, turning out the lantern. "Haven't you had enough of them?"

Nancy was sure she never would have. Soon an intriguing invitation would involve her in another baffling mystery, *The Clue in the Old Album.*

"Anyway," said Ned, "there's one puzzle I wish you would solve for me."

"What's that?"

"Why you always change the subject when I try to talk to you about something that isn't a bit mysterious!"

Nancy smiled and said, "Ned, someday I'll promise to listen."

ORDER FORM

NANCY DREW MYSTERY SERIES

by Carolyn Keene

55 TITLES AT YOUR BOOKSELLER OR COMPLETE THIS HANDY COUPON AND MAIL TO:

GROSSET & DUNLAP, INC.
P.O. Box 941, Madison Square Post Office, New York, N.Y. 10010

Please send me the Nancy Drew Mystery Book(s) checked below @ $2.95 each, plus 25¢ per book postage and handling. My check or money order for $_____ is enclosed. (Please do not send cash.)

☐ 1.	Secret of the Old Clock	9501-7
☐ 2.	Hidden Staircase	9502-5
☐ 3.	Bungalow Mystery	9503-3
☐ 4.	Mystery at Lilac Inn	9504-1
☐ 5.	Secret of Shadow Ranch	9505-X
☐ 6.	Secret of Red Gate Farm	9506-8
☐ 7.	Clue in the Diary	9507-6
☐ 8.	Nancy's Mysterious Letter	9508-4
☐ 9.	The Sign of the Twisted Candles	9509-2
☐ 10.	Password to Larkspur Lane	9510-6
☐ 11.	Clue of the Broken Locket	9511-4
☐ 12.	The Message in the Hollow Oak	9512-2
☐ 13.	Mystery of the Ivory Charm	9513-0
☐ 14.	The Whispering Statue	9514-9
☐ 15.	Haunted Bridge	9515-7
☐ 16.	Clue of the Tapping Heels	9516-5
☐ 17.	Mystery of the Brass Bound Trunk	9517-3
☐ 18.	Mystery at Moss-Covered Mansion	9518-1
☐ 19.	Quest of the Missing Map	9519-X
☐ 20.	Clue in the Jewel Box	9520-3
☐ 21.	The Secret in the Old Attic	9521-1
☐ 22.	Clue in the Crumbling Wall	9522-X
☐ 23.	Mystery of the Tolling Bell	9523-8
☐ 24.	Clue in the Old Album	9524-6
☐ 25.	Ghost of Blackwood Hall	9525-4
☐ 26.	Clue of the Leaning Chimney	9526-2
☐ 27.	Secret of the Wooden Lady	9527-0

☐ 28.	The Clue of the Black Keys	9528-9
☐ 29.	Mystery at the Ski Jump	9529-7
☐ 30.	Clue of the Velvet Mask	9530-0
☐ 31.	Ringmaster's Secret	9531-9
☐ 32.	Scarlet Slipper Mystery	9532-7
☐ 33.	Witch Tree Symbol	9533-5
☐ 34.	Hidden Window Mystery	9534-3
☐ 35.	Haunted Showboat	9535-1
☐ 36.	Secret of the Golden Pavilion	9536-X
☐ 37.	Clue in the Old Stagecoach	9537-8
☐ 38.	Mystery of the Fire Dragon	9538-6
☐ 39.	Clue of the Dancing Puppet	9539-4
☐ 40.	Moonstone Castle Mystery	9540-8
☐ 41.	Clue of the Whistling Bagpipes	9541-6
☐ 42.	Phantom of Pine Hill	9542-4
☐ 43.	Mystery of the 99 Steps	9543-2
☐ 44.	Clue in the Crossword Cipher	9544-0
☐ 45.	Spider Sapphire Mystery	9545-9
☐ 46.	The Invisible Intruder	9546-7
☐ 47.	The Mysterious Mannequin	9547-5
☐ 48.	The Crooked Banister	9548-3
☐ 49.	The Secret of Mirror Bay	9549-1
☐ 50.	The Double Jinx Mystery	9550-5
☐ 51.	Mystery of the Glowing Eye	9551-3
☐ 52.	The Secret of the Forgotten City	9552-1
☐ 53.	The Sky Phantom	9553-X
☐ 54.	The Strange Message in the Parchment	9554-8
☐ 55.	Mystery of Crocodile Island	9555-6

SHIP TO:

NAME _____

(please print)

ADDRESS _____

CITY _____ STATE _____ ZIP _____

Printed in U.S.A.   **Please do not send cash.**